Cousins' Club

Cousins' Club

Warren Alexander

To my Mother and Father
To Andrea

Acknowledgments

I would like to thank my friend Cliff Conner many times. Cliff is an author, professor, historian, and warrior against junk and fake science. His comments in the past were responsible for some the best ideas in the book.

I would like to thank my late friend Stuart Tower, author, lecturer, researcher, veteran, and the patriarch of a most interesting family. His boundless encouragement and whips on the back of a donkey were extremely helpful. In addition, I would like to thank Teresa Chan, George Fisher, Susan Biderman Montez, Alan Drucker, Mark Waters and Gina Araujo for their unconditional support.

I apologize to those who were omitted but offered succor and reassurance but were not specifically mentioned.

But most of all I would like to thank Andrea, my wife of the last two thousand years.

Contents

1

Picking the Bones

No strangers lurked near her casket or behind the hedges. No apparent or misbegotten fortune hunters. The only people not paid to be at Rose Hips's funeral were the family members my grandmother had either cajoled or embarrassed into attending. None of them knew how to contact her sole child, Flora, missing for many years. The gravedigger could have been her ex-husband, a man no one had seen in decades. And now, they each measured how somber they should act.

"She probably died of a sex disease," said Cousin Muriel.

"Quiet. You don't want the rabbi to hear you. He might put it in his eulogy."

"She died of a heart attack, like you're supposed to," said my grandmother Ida of her sister.

But Rose Hips, known for whistling for cabs with her pinkies tucked in the corners of her mouth, seemed too vigorous to have died from a common heart attack. Her very nickname, Rose Hips, arose from the way she danced. She moved with such abandon that her hips did not appear to be attached to her body. If she had not been wearing clothes, they would have flown from her body and circled the room. This was wildly different than the adult who as a shy girl and so thin there didn't seem to be room enough for her intestines.

Later in life, there had been hints and rumors that Rose Hips had been involved with all sorts of men, shadows who disappeared leaving only stories without references. Some suspected she danced the hoochie-coochie, as Fern would say, with anyone. Negroes. Commies. Anyone. Rose Hips knew people talked about her, and she thought that was acceptable.

She would remain out of communication with her family for long periods of time. Her most famous and longest spell without seeing anyone or even a letter came between the wars. Years later, she insinuated that she had spent that time in Paris and was a confidante of Hemingway and Gertrude Stein. But she spoke no French, was not a real or wannabe writer or painter, and knew nothing of philosophy, whether it be simple or pretentious. Some speculated that she posed nude, although no one had seen such a painting. There are always those who think the worst. But most thought that she had spent those years somewhere in Brooklyn and simply wanted to be left alone.

Fortunately, the family had engaged an experienced and glib rabbi to preside over the funeral. When no one could offer gentle anecdotes or information that did not require confirmation, the rabbi invoked every cliché he could muster. A verb. A pronoun. An adjective. Mad Libs for the dead.

At the conclusion of the service, Cousin Yudel whispered to his wife, Fern, "Let's ransack her apartment now."

"Show some respect. We should sit *shiva* first."

"We have a whole week for that, and I'm afraid someone might get there before us."

"Did you see anybody?"

"No. That's what bothers me."

Yudel turned to my father. "We have to ransack the apartment now."

"Shouldn't we sit shiva first?"

"Sure. Later. But first we have to lose the rabbi."

"OK. But we're not going to ransack the place. Just look."

"Sure."

"Thank you, Rabbi," Fern said. "It was very touching. Call me if you need a recommendation."

"That was very good. You should be a full-time rabbi. Somewhere," Cousin Tummler said.

"From now on when I think of death, Rabbi, I will think of you," my mother said.

My grandmother had the "just-in-case" key for Rose Hips's apartment, allowing the family to tiptoe in. An awkward *danse macabre.* Although they all had seen Rose Hips lowered into the ground just hours before, a few feared that they might find her dead again or gently napping on her couch.

"I hear voices," Fern said.

"Voices? No, no. It's the radio." Which was still playing softly, its wooden cabinet warm from being on continuously for days.

"This apartment is nice. I wonder if it's rent-controlled," Muriel said.

"You know, people read obituaries just so they'll know when apartments are available," my father said.

"I would hate to move into a dead person's apartment."

"How do you know you haven't?"

Rose Hips's apartment was neither musty nor perfect. Nothing was frayed or old or smelled like an old woman. They had expected it to be dark, with a faint hint of the unworldly, but the window shades were high and white, allowing the sunlight to brighten the room. The walls were adorned with a few Maxfield Parrish prints plus a few family photos, each perfectly framed, most perfectly square. It all seemed a step above her situation.

"No pictures of Herb, the bastard."

Everyone claimed to have met Rose Hips's ex-husband Herb at least once, somewhere, sometime, but no one remembers the circumstances, what he looked like, or even whether he wore his pants high or baggy. Depending on with whom you gossiped, Herb was either a drunk, a gambler, a philanderer, a fraud, or a Yankees fan. No one could even recall his last name, not surprising after a marriage that lasted such a short time—seconds, it seemed. And Rose Hips always used her maiden name, a rebellious choice for her time.

"Look. Here's a picture of Flora. Do you think she looks like Rose Hips?"

"How old was Rose Hips, Aunt Ida?"

"Aunt Hilda would know, if she was alive."

"How about a guess?"

"A hundred forty-seven."

"Maybe we'll find something with her birth date. If we don't, we'll just make something up for the headstone. No one will know but us."

"Or care."

When my grandmother and her sisters arrived in America, they had no idea when they were born. There were no records. In fact, records were often used against them and were to be avoided. The sisters randomly chose American holidays for birthdays and spread them out over various months so there would be celebrations throughout the year. My grandmother picked Columbus Day, Hilda settled on the Fourth of July, and Hattie selected Arbor Day. No one knew exactly what Arbor Day commemorated, but there were no national holidays in the spring. Rose Hips chose Lincoln's Birthday because it celebrated the birth of our ugliest president.

"I wonder if Rose Hips had a will."

"So how much money do you think she had?"

"The only thing she had was a sex disease from one of those sailors she entertained," Muriel said.

"*Genug* with the sex diseases."

There weren't enough seats for everyone in a tiny apartment of a Lilliputian elderly single woman who lived alone for many years. My blind grandfather, who still had a bit of mud stuck to his shoes from the visit to the cemetery and dinner, found a spot on a petite couch along with the smaller of the women. They settled back comfortably, their heads resting on yellowed antimacassars.

"Before anyone looks for anything, listen to me," Yudel said. "I know these things. People hide stuff where they think other people won't look. But I know. So, someone look in the freezer for jewelry. Don't be fooled. If the package says chicken, it could be diamonds. Steak

4

could be bracelets. Also look on the underside of drawers for envelopes taped there that might have money or savings bonds. And don't forget the backside of the drawer to see if there are envelopes taped there. OK, everybody got it? And remember, you don't know what you're looking for."

No one actually accepted a specific assignment but everyone, save my grandfather, spread out to search the apartment. There were no treasure maps, but that did not diminish their hopes. Some slammed drawers and closets, while others were gentler when opening and closing them, ever respectful of the dead.

"Look at what's in this drawer," said my grandmother. It was filled with matchbooks from various Manhattan and Brooklyn nightclubs. That did not surprise her until one flipped open. She read to herself the handwritten notations on the inside covers. Ben Maksik's Town and Country-Pocket Vito 9. Then another. Cotton Club-Patrick 9. And more. The Elegante-VTH 10, El Morocco-Rocky Times Bastard 0, and Copacabana-Mickey 7. My grandmother was unsure what it all meant but knew it wasn't good. A few had phone numbers.

"Just matchbooks," my grandmother said to no one in particular as she threw several into her purse.

"I feel like a *dybbuk*," said my mother.

"A dybbuk only attaches itself to live people to possess them, not to dead people. They look for live people who are incomplete," my father said, trying to reassure her.

"Incomplete? What the hell does that mean?" asked Yudel.

"It means, they have a hole in their soul."

"What the hell is a hole in your soul?"

"It's like the hole in your *schmekel*, only higher."

My father became mesmerized with Rose Hips's television, as if it were the center of all things wonderful and alien. The television was a heavy piece of compact furniture with a bulbous screen and dials the size of small apple pies. He managed to push it away from the wall and yelled, "I'm checking for money in the TV, like you said."

He stuck his head into the back, searching for greater wisdom, and found a browned, crispy paper schematic, toasted from the heat of the crude vacuum tubes. The diagram showed the position and the model number of the diodes, pentodes, and tetrodes but not their function. Although he didn't know a single program on the air, my father coveted the television set.

Tummler watched all of this and said, "You gotta turn it on." Which he did, while my father's head was still inside.

"That was not very clever. I could have been electrocuted or gone deaf."

The sound of the TV attracted everyone.

"How could she afford a TV?" my mother asked.

"So that's what the note I found means," said Fern, " 'Enjoy the TV. Love VTH.' "

"Who the hell is VTH?"

"I knew she couldn't afford a TV. She was just a bookkeeper."

"But whatta bookkeeper."

"I wonder who she kept the books for."

They all drifted away again to complete the task at hand: greed. The crescendo of slamming doors and drawers again filled the apartment. They mostly found necessities: neatly folded clothes, spare pillows and blankets, and one or two overused pots.

"What are we going to do with all this stuff?"

"We'll divide it between us. Who else's going to take it, Temple Beth *Dreck*?"

"God is going to strike you dead 'cause you say those things. He's going to strike you dead, so say those things in the hall. Away from me," Muriel said.

"She would have wanted her things to go to a Jewish organization."

"How come people always know what dead people want, when they didn't know what they wanted when they were alive?"

"Boy, do I know what she wanted when she was alive," Muriel said.

"We better finish cleaning out the apartment by the thirtieth so we won't have to pay an extra month's rent."

"Screw the landlord. Let him evict a dead woman."

"Maybe we can keep the apartment and use it as clubhouse?"

"Who are you, Mickey Rooney?"

"She was a bookkeeper. She must have money or bank accounts somewhere," said Yudel. He took out his black pocketknife, the one with all sorts of gadgets including a small screwdriver, and started to remove the face plate from an electric switch. "Ha," he barked. He had found a wad of cash among the old coarsely insulated wires.

"How do you know about that?"

"I just know."

My mother meanwhile had rooted around a closet and found three metal boxes. My father helped her take them down and then called to the others, "Come here."

"Is that a good 'come here' or a 'Someone-else-is-dead' come here?"

"Just come here."

They all bent over the three metal boxes, each a different size and color.

"What's in them?"

"How the hell do I know?"

With great anticipation of secrets to be revealed and untold treasures, they realized they didn't have keys. The locks looked like they could be opened with an angry glare. They all stared silently at the boxes as if their concentrated power would make them pop open.

"Has anyone tried this?" With that, my grandmother simply opened the top of one. It was unlocked and exploded with decades of yellow receipts from money orders for the rent, gas, electric, and phone.

"Smart," said Yudel, "No checking account; no trail for the tax man."

But the lid for the largest box would not open. Yudel jimmied it open with the side of a blade.

"Watch it! Don't cut anything."

Everyone's eyebrows furrowed in confusion except Fern's, whose eyebrows arched in recognition of the contents.

"What the hell are those things?"

"They look like kitchen thingamajigs."

"Some are just rubber," said Tummler, holding one up to the light to inspect it. "But not this one."

By now they all were fingering them and turning them upside down with quizzical looks.

"This one seems like you could use it to unclog a drain. Here, let me plug it in."

Fern, who had been silent up to now, yelped, "Don't."

"Why not?"

"Just don't."

Among the objects were yellowed and tattered pages from Sears catalogs and *Home Needlework Journals*. Fern took one of the magazines and read aloud for all to hear, "All the pleasures of youth... will throb within you."

"So what does that mean?" asked my grandmother.

"Here, from Sears," Fern read from the *Wish Book*. " 'An aid every *woman* appreciates,' " she said, emphasizing the word *woman*.

"Maybe we should put these things down."

"They help women feel better," Fern said.

"They're for sex!" Fern's husband, Yudel, said. "How come you know about these sex things?"

"Maybe I should get one," said one of the other women.

"And they're old. Look at the dates on the magazines. April 1926. Look, that one has dust on it."

"Thank God."

"She's had them for twenty-five years."

"And she bought them before the Depression."

"People were happier then."

"There are secrets and then there are secrets," my mother said. "Let's open the last box and hope for the best."

"Aha, this is what we've been looking for." Everyone grabbed something. There was jewelry, savings bonds, and cash, some of which was in little red envelopes that the Chinese give as gifts on joyous occasions to unmarried people with the hope they would not need the little red envelopes the following year.

"Why couldn't she have cash like normal people?"

"Look! Here's an envelope from Flora," my mother said, "but it's empty."

"What's the postmark?"

"Los Alamos, New Mexico."

"Isn't that where Davy Crockett died?"

"That's not good," said my father. "That's where they had those atomic bomb tests."

"Maybe she was a nuclear scientist?"

"She did things with her fingers," said Tummler.

"You mean sew?"

The family had long been enthralled by Flora's various skills. But her true talent was creating itchy, fringy cushions inscribed with sayings such as "The Seven Pillows of Wisdom," "Pillow of Strength," or just the word "Talk."

Before her inexplicable disappearance, she was working on interchangeable word pillows. A few in the family thought that, no matter how talented she was, she was asking too much money for her products. Fern thought that if Flora had asked for less money and stayed in Brooklyn, she would be alive today. She departed to sell her wares to that most American of retail establishments, the gift shop, and on that trip, disappeared somewhere in the United States. Well, maybe she was alive. Or maybe she was dead. It's always difficult to prove nonexistence.

"OK," said my grandmother. "Let's finish up."

"What are we going to do next?"

"I'll take the rubber things home and throw them out from my home," Fern said.

"I'll take the jewelry to that *gonif* Cohen on Fulton Street and see what I can get," said my grandmother. "We'll meet Tuesday night at my house and see how much money we have. And then we'll decide what to do with it."

"We're going to keep it, right?"

"What are we going to do about the TV?" my father asked.

"We'll share it," Yudel said.

"The money or the TV?"

"And how are you going to share a TV?" my father asked.

"You can watch some stations. I can watch the other ones. I'll take it first," Yudel said.

Just as they were ready to leave, Muriel bent her head and nodded. "You know, Flora was a genius."

"Yeah, it takes a genius to do what she did," said Fern.

"But she won't be the only genius in the family," said my grandmother with a furious mix of indignation, bluster, envy, and the realization that she was the last surviving sister.

2

The Discussion

Rose Hips's life covered my grandmother's kitchen table. The family threw into a pile whatever clothing of hers they had as if they intended to do a laundry later. They separated her papers into little piles, applying their own individual logic. Savings bonds, which were easily identifiable, became their own pile. They sifted through a green mound of ones searching for fives and tens. They even found a can opener.

"Aunt Ida, how much did you get for the jewelry?"

My grandmother nearly giggled. "I went to Cohen on Fulton Street and got four hundred and seventy-four dollars," said my grandmother. "Then I went next door to A&S to get one of those square ice cream cones. But I paid for that myself."

"That means it must be worth two grand if that gonif Cohen gave you that much," Yudel said.

"Are you finished counting the money?"

"What's this?" asked Unkle Traktor as he held up a piece of paper between his thumb and index finger as if he were throwing out something with dog shit on it.

"*Guttenyu!*" said Muriel, "It's Rose Hips's Republican voter registration card."

"Republican," hissed Unkle Traktor. Then with a wet and crude spitting sound created by pursing his lips like a grouper and showing the tip of his tongue, he expelled a loud *phaaaaaa*, accompanied by a single violent shake of his head.

"It's a good thing she's dead already. Because if you're Republican, I don't think you can be buried in a Jewish cemetery."

My grandmother had invited her other daughter, Aunt Georgia, and her husband, Unkle Traktor.

"Big deal! So she was a Republican," Yudel said.

"Who knows how and where she got this money," said Unkle Traktor.

"We can't take it. It's like using medical research from Josef Mengele."

"You would use Mengele's research if it cured you of whatever you had."

"What do you expect from a Trotskyite?" Muriel asked.

"I've told you a million times, I'm not a Trotskyite, I'm a Trotskyist. It's the difference between a socialite and a socialist," Unkle Traktor said.

"Ist, ite, ite, ist. You're still a Commie know-it-all. So what does it add up to?" asked Muriel.

Aunt Georgia and Unkle Traktor weren't as much outcasts as the others were tired of the constant and narrow prism by which the two of them viewed the world.

"Shouldn't we have asked the other Roses to help with the decision?" asked my mother.

"No. They're all a pain in the ass. They don't deserve nothing."

There were many Roses in the family. In fact, when my grandmother told my grandfather that Rose had died, he asked which one. We needed nicknames to properly sort them. There was Joe's Rose, Willie's Rose, Nose Rose, White Rose (she dyed her mustache), and Meatball Rose. Meatball Rose made just enough meatballs to give every guest two each and not one piece of fat more.

Many had two nicknames: one for public consumption and one for private amusement. Nose Rose, who had worked in notions at a department store, measured ribbon by holding it to the tip of her nose and stretching it to the end of her longest finger. She was also known as Rose Bust. Her cleavage started just under her neck and could be viewed even if she wore a turtleneck. She enticed unsuspecting little children with a hug into that quicksand of flesh known as her chest, where they quickly vanished.

Meatball Rose was also known as Suppose Rose. She was so cheap, her name became part of an insult. Suppose she actually gave you a gift you wanted? You suppose she kisses other people's *mezuzahs* before she enters her apartment so she doesn't wear out her own.

Willie's Rose took great umbrage when someone named their parrot Aunt Rose. She took this as a personal slight. It was difficult to realize her specific complaint since her green-and-yellow dresses resembled plumage, and her false teeth chattered as if cracking nuts.

Joe's Rose, who was not trustworthy and was a *yenta* of the first order, was also known as Tokyo Rose. The problem with people like Tokyo Rose was that although they might know some interesting things, they insisted on telling you everything else first.

But none of these Roses sat among them today, except the dead one.

"So how much do we have altogether?"

"I don't know. We're still adding it up."

"And you never know how they figure those bonds," my father said. "Look at the way they're typed. None of the letters line up. Who can read that?"

"So what should we do with the money?"

"Let's just split it up."

"We should give to those who need it," Aunt Georgia said.

"Yeah. Us."

"We could all go to the Catskills."

"I'll go to Las Vegas and play craps at Bugsy Siegel's place. I know somebody who knows somebody. I can double my money," Yudel said.

"I think we should have a party."

"What are we, the Donners?"

"No. The Donners gave a party, but no one brought food. That's why they ate each other."

"So when do we eat?"

"Ida, don't feed these *schnorrers* until we decide what to do with the money," my grandfather said. "And no drinks either, until someone says something smart."

"We could thirst to death."

"For once in your life, someone say something smart," said my grandfather. "No eating until then. God damn it."

No one could recall my grandfather exerting such authority, cursing, or even displaying that level of anger or urgency. His sense of mortality must have seeped through.

"I have an invention. With the money, I can get a patent and put it into production," my father said.

"Another brilliant invention from Edison here. What is it this time? A light bulb that only works during the day?" said Muriel.

"We can open a franchise, like a Howard Johnson," said Tummler.

"Too *goyisha*."

"I like the idea of a franchise," said Unkle Traktor. "It's a word whose origin means liberty."

"Arthur Murray Dance Studios is a franchise."

"Even more goyisha."

"We'll make it Jewish. We'll teach the cha-cha."

"This has gotta stop."

"What's gotta stop?"

"None of you has ever done nothing."

"What are you talking about?"

"Just what I said. None of you have ever done nothing."

"We have must done something, sometime," said my father.

"None of you have ever done nothing. Never. *Gornisht. Gornisht helfin.*"

"You have to be the stupidest Jewish family in America." Blaming others was my grandmother's idea of introspection.

"That can't be true. There must be someone stupider than us," said Yudel.

"Then you find them," said my grandmother.

"We're not stupid. We are deciding our future. So can we eat now?"

It wasn't that the family was stupid. It was that they just weren't very smart. They pulled the front door when it needed to be pushed. They tried to get in the side door when there was none. And they tried to escape by the back door but were not sure why they were running.

"But this is all going to change," said my grandmother. "Remember the other day I said something about a genius?"

"Yeah. So?"

"Well, I went to the library today. And the *Gematria* agrees with me." My grandmother stood erect and with a gray certitude in her eye, added, "The next child born into this family will be a genius."

"Since when do you know the *Gematria*?"

"What kind of nonsense is that, the next child will be a genius?"

"I always knew the *Gematria*," my grandmother said. "But this time, I added up all the dates of our birthdays and our ages, and the *Gematria* says that the next baby born into this family will be a genius."

The *Gematria* revelation and my grandmother's harsh assessment of the family's intellectual ability were greeted with knitted brows and skewed mouths. Until this moment, no one knew that my grandmother had this latent talent and knowledge, let alone was able to articulate it.

"By the way, what the hell is the *Gematria*?" asked someone for everyone.

"You don't know what the *Gematria* is?"

"It's a Hebrew system of reckoning by numbers rooted in mysticism. The height of its popularity occurred back in Spain between the eleventh and thirteenth centuries," my father said. "It gives random numbers meaning. But I always thought it was highly inexact."

"That could be true," Yudel said. "You know how we give gifts in increments of eighteen for chai? Chai is the eighteenth letter of the Hebrew alphabet and means life."

"Well, that's the *Gematria*, too. Right?" Tummler said.

"And what is the total amount of money we have again?" asked my grandmother.

"Do we have a final figure yet?"

"Four hundred seventy-four in jewelry, three hundred sixty-three in cash money, and a hundred ninety-five in bonds."

"What does that add up to?"

"A thousand thirty-four," said my father without the use of a pencil and paper.

"Show off."

"And that number, according to the *Gematria*, means we will all be rich one day," said my grandmother."

"Aunt Ida, one question," asked Fern. "What the hell are you talking about? One day, we're stupid. Then *poof*, the next day we're rich."

"It's complicated," explained my grandmother. "Each number means something different, but when you add them up, it means we'll be rich. And the next born will be the genius who will make us rich."

"That *Gematria* has an answer for everything," said Muriel.

"That's crazy," said Unkle Traktor. "You just can't make up stuff and expect us to believe it."

"OK, Mr. Bigmouth. Tell us why it isn't true."

"You just can't believe mystical mumbo jumbo. How do you refute mumbo jumbo?"

"I don't know. We've been trying to do that to you for years."

My grandmother could not have asked for a better comment, because whatever Unkle Traktor was for, the family was against, and whatever Unkle Traktor was against… And he was against everything.

"I'm pregnant," said my mother with the reluctance of a confession.

"You weren't pregnant yesterday," said Fern.

"I'm pregnant," my mother repeated.

"What, you *shtupped* right after the funeral?"

"I'm almost three months pregnant."

"Some coincidence. Aunt Ida says the next baby's going to be a genius, and the next baby is her first grandchild."

"You knew, Aunt Ida."

"We trusted you, Aunt Ida."

My grandmother had to restore belief in her and her prediction and quell the uprising. "But," my grandmother added, "Since my daughter and Danny are not smart enough to raise a genius by themselves, we will pass the baby around from house to house."

"What?" said my father.

"Everybody, everybody will have a part in raising this genius, and we'll teach him everything we know."

My grandmother continued, "Every year, we'll pass the child along to the next family so they can teach it what they know. And so on and so forth. That way we know it'll be a genius."

My mother started to cry. "What are talking about? How can you take my baby away?" I am not sure why my mother cried as she had yet to meet me.

"It's not your baby, it's everybody's baby. It's a genius, and you're being selfish. It will be good for the child. And you must help the entire family."

"You can't do that," said my father.

This was a complete turnaround from just a few days earlier when my mother told my grandmother she was pregnant. My parents invited her and my grandfather over to the apartment to tell them the good news. But upon learning that my mother was pregnant, my grandmother shrieked that I was going to be mentally deficient.

My grandmother believed that when the electric sockets were not in use, the energy would ooze out on the floor and create huge puddles of invisible danger that could eat through your brain or, in the case of my parents, their sex organs. The remedy was those pronged plastic stoppers that are pressed into the wall socket to prevent children from sticking in their fingers or something like a screwdriver. Although my grandmother had been in America for over fifty years, you cannot take the girl out of the bleak and muddy *shtetl*. But now the circumstances were different.

"I don't want to raise someone else's kid, even if he is a genius," Fern said.

"That is one crazy-ass idea," said Tummler.

"You can't do this," said my mother.

"You're all being selfish," said my grandmother, "It just so happens Dot is the next one who's pregnant. If Fern, Muriel, or God forbid, my other daughter was pregnant, that baby would be the genius. No one is smart enough to raise a genius by themselves. Look at all of you. Traktor, he knows things no one else cares about. Tummler hanging out with other comedians who aren't funny either. Yudel with his gangster friends. Or my son-in-law with his *fakakta* inventions."

My grandmother simply wanted to change the fate of the family, and it was obvious that those present could not do it on their own. And if her attempts to change this should turn out to be misguided, the best anyone could do is curse her memory.

"So we're all gonna have the baby?" Yudel asked.

"That doesn't make no sense."

"What are we going to tell the neighbors?" asked Muriel.

"Conformity is a form of fear," said Unkle Traktor.

"What does that have to do with what the neighbors think?" asked Muriel.

"We'll use this money to help defray some expenses. We'll call it the Genius Fund, and I'll take care of it," said my grandmother.

"But City College is free."

"He may go out of town. You have to pay if he goes out of town."

"How do we know it's a he?"

"You never know what types of expenses you get before he gets to college."

"Then we'll call it the Republican Genius Fund," said Unkle Traktor.

"No, we'll call it the Republican Genius Dildo Fund," said Yudel, casting an angry glare toward Fern.

"I told you, I threw them out," Fern said.

"It doesn't matter," said Yudel.

"How will we know if the baby is a genius?"

Hair," said Muriel. "If it has hair like Einstein, then you know it's a genius."

"But all babies have hair like Einstein."

"OK, but what if it's born with a mustache?"

"You mean like White Rose?"
And that is how my future was decided.

3

First Memories

Thus, I was born moments after the twentieth century cracked in half. At least numerically. I had already enthusiastically accepted my grandmother's challenge to be a genius while in utero. If I failed to be a genius, then I would simply be another family failure, if not a spectacular one. But if I succeeded, I would offer hope after centuries of ill luck and worse fortune.

Before the abrupt and random prophesy, my mother's pregnancy was as uneventful and clinical as the drab gestation charts displayed in high school hygiene classes. But the prediction turned her phone into a constant source of obvious and repetitious questions. My mother's response was unreasonably calm and restrained. All asked with an undercurrent of anxiety, confusion about their future role, and greed. Some made empty gestures.

"How's our little genius today?"

"What did the doctor say? Is there anything I can do for you?"

Muriel always added, "You know, he's not the first genius in the family." Of course, my mother understood Muriel's implied insult referred to Second or Third Cousin Flora.

When my parents took me home from the hospital, the family wisely decided they did not want to explain to the doctors and the staff what was about to happen. Yet at the *bris*, everyone was shocked by how affable and agreeable, even resigned to the arrangement, my parents had become. Their transformation was sudden and had many possible explanations. Maybe it was the burden of the constant care and attention of taking care of a baby. Maybe they did not want to continually argue with the family and my grandmother, although arguing about nothing gave the family a common purpose. Arguing about something that actually had consequences was nearly virgin territory. Or maybe my parents were afraid of the responsibility of raising a genius solely by themselves.

The *mohel* was an unsuspecting accomplice who unintentionally perfected the deal. My parents handed me to him. He performed the centuries old ceremonial cut. Then he handed me back to my grandmother for comforting, making it appear official.

Men always, either literally or emotionally, grab their crotch at the bloodiest moment of a bris. Everyone was surprised that I did not cry or scream during the entire rite. Later I was told that I just looked the mohel in eye with a determined expression as if to say, "Will you do this fast?"

"He is either the bravest baby I have ever seen or the stupidest," was the general sentiment of all the gathered. But once the mohel finished, those in attendance stormed the wall of sponge cake and drained the moat of warm soda and cheap sweet wine.

It was not that my grandmother was the most knowledgeable about raising children, but she knew things the longest, even if her skills had to be dusted off and polished. Yet staying with her seemed like the most natural and least offensive initial choice.

My grandparents' apartment was perfect for a child for another unusual reason. My grandfather was blind, and the entire apartment was soft and slow. The chairs were heavily cushioned, the tables round without corners. There were no rugs to slip on, just carpeting, and the wooden floor saddles lay smooth and low. There were no glass cabinets or *tchotchkes* on tables to knock over as my grandfather used his hands like antennae, slightly extended from his body, feeling, stretching for what was there yesterday. He even liked soft food, like cereal saturated in milk, cold fish, and the insides of bread.

He had been left totally blind in a botched operation in an era when it was an affront to sue a doctor for malfeasance. The doctor, however, gave my grandparents money in return for the sole promise that they would forget his name. They used the money to buy a house, commonly called a "taxpayer." The first two floors could be rented legally, while the one in the basement was strictly paid for in cash.

My grandfather looked like Stan Laurel, wore an Oliver Hardy mustache, but never did a double take, let alone a triple take. He read braille the way a freshman speaks French, with hesitation, as his fingers came upon the raised dots. The term in braille for where no dots are in the configuration of characters is an "empty cell."

My grandfather's blindness did not really bother him. It reaffirmed his view of the world as a dark narrow tunnel with few escapes. It did, however, affect his ideas on raising children. He had forgotten all the lessons of being a parent and would say things to me like, "Stop acting like a baby."

He did teach me the value of inertia. The lesson was one of example rather than a formal application of physics. He clung motionless to a corner of the sofa, the floor bore the weight of his feet, one arm dangled from the arm of the couch, and the other lay limp by his side while his head created a grease spot on the wall that grew darker every year. "It's OK to do nothing, as long as it's not the only thing you do," he said often. Occasionally he sang a song only he knew.

I am not sure how my grandparents met nor what was the attraction. I never asked and could only speculate now. They could have met in steerage on the way to America. But my grandfather was born here. They could have met in high school. But my grandfather never attended high school. It could have been that my grandmother was easy to spot.

At a time when three grandmothers needed to stand on each other's shoulders to do the dishes, my grandmother stood tall at five feet ten. She was at once proud of and self-conscious about her height and called her mah-jongg friends the Pygmies of Ellis Island.

Still, she worried that her height created an angle that hindered her cooking style. She said that her height was like preventing a pigeon from swooping down on a mouse from high in the sky. For those reasons, she cut off part of the handles from her wooden spoons. She bent the metal spatulas that she used to flip her *latkes* because she claimed it gave her better leverage. No matter. She believed it helped her feed us and that pigeons swooped. As she aged, she shrank, as most do, and measured herself against the wall with tick marks, like parents who chronicle a child's growth, but in reverse. As the pencil lines got lower and lower, she felt more comfortable around people.

My paternal grandparents were mislaid somewhere on the long stretch of cemeteries on the Brooklyn-Queens border. An area once endless with farms was now littered with hearses and tombstones. Even though there are plenty of Jewish cemeteries, they could have been buried in a nondenominational graveyard. My father wasn't sure. He, who knew where Houdini and Bernard Baruch were buried, could never find his keys or his parents.

I was swaddled in Jewish superstitions. I did not have a true name until after I was born. A centuries-old superstition was revived especially for my birth. As ignorance has it, an unborn baby was given a false name until the bris, so the Angel of Death would not know the true identity of the baby and kill him. Apparently, the Angel of Death was only interested in killing boy babies.

Thus, I was accorded the name Nebuchadnezzar, more precisely Nebuchadnezzar II. According to the Bible, my namesake conquered Jerusalem and forced the Jews into exile. He destroyed the First Temple but, in a moment of ethereal balance, created the Hanging Gardens of Babylon. How better to fool the Angel of Death than to be named for someone Jews hated and who hated the Jews? This arcane ruse must have been conceived by either my father or Aunt Esther, for no one else in the family knew these details, let alone how to pronounce Nebuchadnezzar.

All this to outsmart something that didn't even exist. And if he did exist, why couldn't the Angel of Death kill me after the bris? And how come he hadn't figured out the ploy after hundreds of years?

Another superstition led to my disfigurement. That one forbids the purchase of furniture or gifts until a baby is born. Again, it was to fool the Angel of Death by concealing one's good fortune before the birth. Unlike the baby-naming diversion, this tradition is still practiced.

I slept in a drawer for the first weeks of my existence until a proper crib could be purchased and, more important, assembled. For my blind grandfather, this open drawer was akin to rearranging the furniture, and one evening he slammed the drawer shut, breaking the distal phalanx of my *digitus medius manus* or the top of my fuck-you finger. The tip of my tiny finger thereafter made a permanent left turn, a unique characteristic of which I remain proud.

When I became older and I gave people the finger, whether intentionally or unintentionally, most did not know to whom I was pointing. This invariably led to fights, more out of confusion than animosity. And the beginning of a fight provides a poor forum to explain a Jewish tradition gone awry. My only real problem with my misdirected finger was finding winter, baseball, and hockey gloves. Since I could not put my fingers in my hockey glove, I borrowed a ploy and cut out the palm. I would stick my hand through the hole and could do all sorts of things without the referee detecting them, like holding or jabbing the other players. People often said my finger was a conversation piece, but I do not believe in conversation pieces. Either you have something to say, or you do not. And if you do not have something to say, why would you want to say it with your finger?

Even with a historical or religious context, most superstitions do not make sense. For instance the superstition that you must never sew clothes when someone is wearing them. And if you do, make sure you chew string. It was thought that the stitches would close your brain and not allow the common sense out. One of the more ironic superstitions, and it makes one wonder about Jews being the people of Einstein, Salk, and Oppenheimer.

My grandmother would read to me, not from standard children's books, but from letters and responses in the popular column called the *Bintel Brief* (Yiddish for bundle of letters) found in influential daily newspaper the *Forward* (the *Forverts*). The column started at the beginning of the twentieth century when poor and lonely Jewish immigrants wrote to the asking for advice. The questions could be about matters of the heart, although most were concerned with how to be a good socialist and freethinker or how to handle knotty daily problems. But even as the fortunes of Jews grew and many assimilated, the need for advice continued.

Some days my grandmother read yellowed clippings that she had saved for years, while other times she would read directly from that day's edition. When she read the questions regarding love, she often punctuated her sentences with sighs and arched her eyebrows as if they were levitating. How clever of my grandmother to read these to me as I learned both Yiddish and complications of adult life.

Yet none of these was my earliest memory. My very first vivid memory occurred one night, when I saw two inky silhouettes in the darkened apartment. One was unmistakably my tall grandmother, but the other was not my grandfather. He walked with confidence, not the tentative steps of a blind man. He walked with a laugh, and my grandmother returned the laugh. All I could see in the shadow was the outline of the world's largest pompadour. The mammoth protuberance harkened his arrival like the revered horn ornament of a 1948 Packard as his greased mound glistened in the light of the *yahrzeit* candle flickering in remembrance of dead ancestors.

They went to a small, sparsely furnished room, one with the tiniest of tables, the dimmest of lamps, and a couch. The house then filled with the appreciative sounds reserved for the efforts of others. Fortunately or unfortunately, my grandfather did not recognize these unseemly sounds for what they were, as they crescendoed and cascaded around every corner of the house. He awoke and yelled out, "Who is that? Get out of my house. I have a gun."

His gun was a butter knife covered in the residue of pot cheese, his favorite food. He stumbled through the house with a look of panic, brandishing the butter knife, and again screaming, "Get out. Get out. I have a gun."

My grandfather swung the knife wildly, leaving a white chevron of pot cheese on the Pompadour's sleeve and cutting a tiny white slit on my grandmother's favorite flocking. The Pompadour, otherwise unharmed, slid down the stairs.

"And don't come back," my grandfather said with finality. Then he asked, "Ida, are you all right?"

Even though my grandfather should have had the advantage in the dark, the Pompadour's quick escape showed that he had been in much worse situations than being chased by a blind man with a butter knife covered in cheese curds.

For all this, I am grateful. At this very young age, I learned the value of stoicism. It is not that I am an acolyte of Zeno of Citium, even though Zeno taught that fortitude would lead to the control of emotions which in turn leads to clear thought. How could I blame a grandmother for seeking companionship? Or an unctuous Lothario for providing that companionship? Or blame a blind man for an accident? Or an ill-trained doctor for not straightening my finger? Or the Angel of Death for what was done in his name?

It is not that I am fearless or impervious to pain and the actions of others. Nor am I a Pollyanna who sees the good in everyone. Nor am I a proselytizing zealot, who thinks he can change others by exposing and exploiting their weaknesses. Mine is a comfortable and pragmatic acceptance that I can change little of what goes on around me. It is not Zeno of Citium on the inside, it is Zeno of Citium on the outside.

4

Yudel and Fern

Just after my first birthday and without fanfare or ceremony, I was handed off to Yudel and Fern. The order for these exchanges had been determined by picking names from a hat. It was a nice hat, at that, the type men wore to work just before and after World War II.

Yudel and Fern owned a grocery store that did not bear a formal name on the outside, just a faded Coca-Cola logo. There was a hand-lettered sign in smudged ink covering most of the front window, declaring, "We Specialize in Everything." On most days, including the winter, my cousins sat outside of the tiny store on old wooden soda crates, waiting for customers.

The grocery business is a tough business, especially when you do not sell much and the margins are thin. When they did make money, they secreted it away in a safety deposit box, as did almost all the local merchants. The store was so dimly lit that it appeared closed. If it were not for a weak bulb near the cash register throwing a yellow cast, even the regulars would not have known it was open.

The floorboards creaked under everyone's soles, and the shelves sagged from age. The ice cream freezer case held brands no one had ever heard of, the type where the paper wrapper sticks to the soggy cone and actually improves the flavor. The porcelain exterior of the refrigerator cases was so badly chipped that it looked like marbling, while the tin ceiling was mottled by cigarette smoke and neglect. But who looks up in a grocery store? They also sold seltzer in the heavy blue bottles with a manacle as a spigot. Beside these stood regular seltzer in bottles that needed a standard bottle opener. This version lacked the carbonation or the body of the blue-bottled seltzer but people had their favorites. Yudel would say, "Club soda is for stains. Tonic water is for rich bastards. But seltzer water grows hair on your balls." Of course, he did not say that to everyone.

Even though they were not religious, Yudel and Fern closed the grocery on Rosh Hashanah and Yom Kippur for the sake of appearance. They hated taking off for the eight days of Passover.

Fern did not see herself as a grocery store owner. She thought she was the Jewish Andrews Sister. She would often sing to the customers, whether they liked it or not. She especially liked "Beat Me, Daddy, Eight to The Bar" and "Bei Mir Bistu Sheyn." At family affairs, she insisted on singing with the bar mitzvah bands. One band intentionally played off-key just to disrupt her vocals. She was always searching for the other Jewish Andrews Sisters to start a group. Yudel, a terrible piano player, liked to accompany Fern. He thought she was pretty good, and she appreciated his effort and support.

The sins of the parents shall befall the son, and so it was for their son, Jerry, the product of their teenage lust. Jerry was sentenced to life at the grocery. He fancied himself a ladies' man and tried to make the most of the one non-grocery fact he knew as a pickup line. "You know," he would say to the women, "soldiers wore chinos during the Spanish-American War, and now I am here to serve you." Before every bike delivery, ignoring history and in constant fits of unearned optimism, he would say, "I could be a while." He always returned quickly.

Jerry's head was ovate like an eggplant. Moments after he shaved, it looked like he needed another. He had a collection of muscle shirts and T-shirts, where he rolled his cigarettes in the short sleeves. Jerry put his comb in the back pocket of his chinos, which made him look like he was shitting nettles. His main job, besides deliveries, was to stock the store, but he refused to use a ladder or reacher-grabber, so every top shelf was a mess. When Yudel or Fern would say something, he would respond, "Women's work." It was always unclear how much Jerry was paid but he was not going anywhere. He was, however, my one-quarter brother for lack of a better name for our relationship.

Since Yudel and Fern both worked, I spent most days at the grocery. Whenever I needed a nap, they would lay me in the "Not for Trade" produce scale and give it a gentle swing. With a bit of padding, the scale was quite comfortable. The customers thought it was cute as long as I did not do anything untoward before their peaches were weighed.

Yudel owed the Boys money because of his gambling habits. Because he was unable to pay off these debts, the Boys used his grocery store as a front for running numbers. Grocery stores and dry cleaners were naturals for the numbers racket. Instead of passing a grocery list over the counter or a receipt for a pressed pair of pants, people would hand over a piece of paper with their selected number and some money for the bet. To win, you had to match your three-digit number with a three-digit number that was impossible to fix or manipulate. Usually, the winning number was the handle, the last three numbers of the total amount bet at a race track, a figure published for everyone to see in the newspapers. This gave credibility to an illegal act.

Often there were knots of bettors waiting for the newspapers to be delivered. Some people never bought the paper but only flipped to the back page to check the handle; others would ask, "Can I just look over your shoulder?"

Yudel loved taking numbers, even though it was supposed to be a punishment for not paying his debts. But he thought it made him a *shtarker*. He used the same type of money clip as many of the Boys, a small but thick rubber band usually reserved for binding broccoli stalks together. Theirs held their large bills in a tight wad. Yudel's was all singles with a ten as the wrapper.

Protection money was collected from every shop owner and Yudel was not an exception. As a kid, I assumed everybody paid protection, even Macy's. Maybe Macy's paid more, and the Boys sent someone important to pick up the cash. Or maybe they paid in pinkie rings from the jewelry counter.

Fern took care of the regular customers, while Yudel saw to the special customers, like the crooks and the beat cop, whom he bribed with food and neighborhood gossip.

But it was the illegal bialys that kept the store profitable. When Yudel and Fern bought the store, they found an oven in the corner of the basement that the certificate of occupancy did not list. The fire marshals never inspected it, although Yudel would have gladly bribed them too, if necessary. The oven was hidden behind a partial brick wall, probably once used for coal storage. Yudel hung a dark tarp to block the view from the top of the stairs and randomly threw empty cartons here and there in the basement to emulate disuse. Of course, he could never figure out a way to disguise the heat of a working oven or the odor of freshly made bialys.

His bialys were spectacular. A bialy savant. The dough was moist, and the outsides were perfectly brown. With his thumb, he pressed little craters in the center, filling some with chopped onion or garlic, leaving others empty. And on Sundays, he made *pletzels*—bialys the size of dinner plates covered in poppy seeds and onions. You would take them home, toast them, slather them with butter and, as all good Jews do, die of a heart attack.

The ingredients could not be simpler: high-gluten flour, salt, ice water, and yeast. Yudel thought the special ingredient was the ice water but he never shared the exact proportions with anyone, including Fern. It was the one thing he did better than others, and he wanted it to stay that way. Jerry, of course, dragged the bags of ice to the basement.

Every Wednesday, exactly at noon, two of the Boys came to the store to collect the vig, the murderous weekly interest charged by loan sharks. One Wednesday, the store was filled by three wide men whose shiny black hair and shiny black shoes were only separated by the dun of their camel hair coats. While Jerry hid behind cartons of Rice Krispies, Fern stuck defiantly to the seat on her soda crate.

"Where's our money, Yudel?"

"What money? I pay on time."

"I'm not talking about the vig."

"Well, what are you talking about?"

"You're skimming money off the top."

"You know I would never do that to you guys."

"Yeah, but your book is behind every other guy who runs numbers in the neighborhood. So either you're a thief or an idiot."

"Then I'm an idiot. You guys know I would never do that."

"You are an idiot, and now you won't be able to pick your nose, too."

With that, they grabbed Yudel and put his right hand in the bread slicer and flipped the switch. His screams could be heard for blocks. But people running into the store saw who it was and ran out just as quickly. When the mobbed-up guys left, one said to no one in particular, "Best thing since sliced bread."

The steel fingers of the machine had removed Yudel's, which now lay among crumbs and rye seeds. Even if he wasn't guilty of theft, it sent a reminder to everyone else in the neighborhood from the mob. "Sometimes you just gotta whack somebody." Or just make it memorable.

* * *

Without half of his fingers, business got worse. No one wanted Yudel to touch their groceries, even packaged goods, but especially anything sliced by hand—meats or cheese. Besides their repulsion, everyone knew who chopped them off and did not want to offend them. Kids would come into the store and ask for a rye bread, sliced, then run out laughing. Another yelled, "Here's my ticket to the Dodgers game, want to see my stub?"

Yudel tried to get worker's compensation and told them he cut off his fingers slicing bread. When the bureaucrat asked for proof, Yudel held up his hand. "I'm going to need more than that," said the bureaucrat.

"Like what?"

"Witnesses. No liars. Pictures. Not touched up. Do you have the fingers? That would be good."

All of this put a burden on Jerry, who after years of working at the grocery still did not know how much bologna to cut or potato salad to spoon out to make a half a pound. And when he ladled too much potato salad into a container, he would eat the extra half spoonful or the extra slices of bologna in front of the customers rather than give it to them in the name of good will.

Unkle Traktor and Aunt Georgia came to visit Yudel and Fern to offer advice and sympathy. Unkle Traktor told Yudel that after Otto von Bismarck tried to destroy the socialists and Marxists, he tried to placate the masses by establishing the first modern disability program.

Yudel replied, "Great. I'll see him first thing Monday."

Aunt Georgia tried to offer cheery history of her own. She pointed out that Paul Wittgenstein, the concert pianist and brother of Ludwig, if you didn't know that, had lost his right arm during World War I. Then the pianist asked famous composers, like Ravel and Prokofiev, to write piano pieces solely for the left hand.

But Yudel had had enough. "Do you think this guy Ravel is still around? If not, what about asking Harry Ruby or Irving Berlin?"

All of this contributed to Yudel's deteriorating state. To prove to himself and the family that he was a protective and worthy father, he would pick me up as often as possible. Unfortunately, many times I would slip through his missing fingers and, a few times, I hit the ground. I tried not to cry. But one day, he dropped me on my face producing a scar between my eyes that looked like the map of Israel. Sort of. I was and am proud of that scar. It's like wearing your emotions on your sleeve, except it's in the middle of your forehead. Of course, most Americans are terrible at geography, and few recognized it for what it was, except for a couple of Jews in the neighborhood and an Israeli cartographer. Yudel, unfortunately, had dropped me on my head before the 1967 Six-Day War, so neither Gaza nor the West Bank were represented.

As business worsened, Fern suggested that they sell his bialy recipe and the equipment to the highest bidder. To entice buyers, Fern and Jerry handed out bite-size crusty bialy bits with a smear of butter. They usually hid Yudel in the basement, but one day when he came up for air, *Chazzer* Cohen happened to be there. The Chazzer saw Yudel and asked, "*Nu*, Mister, you don't like me anymore?"

Yudel was a little taken aback. He had pissed off the Mafia and he certainly did not want to insult the Chazzer, even though his name meant *pig* in Yiddish.

"Of course I like you. Who wouldn't?"

The Chazzer was too rich to live in the neighborhood but did. Everyone had a different opinion as to the source of his wealth. The story with the most currency speaks of when the Chazzer owned a newsstand in Times Square. Hookers would bring him money from different countries, and he would give them US dollars at a premium. But now, he was too rich to stand in the cold with the fingertips of his woolen gloves cut off for handling money more easily. He still maintained his underground money exchange and the newsstand and who knew what else.

Many were afraid of the tentacles of power that money brings, although no one could recall an episode involving the Chazzer that might evoke such fear. He wore a sweater in the summer and the same coat every day in the winter. No one knew his real first name and most doubted that he had a wife and children. No one had been to his apartment nor had he been to theirs.

"I hear you are selling your bialy recipe, and you didn't ask me," said the Chazzer.

"You're a busy, important man."

"What, suddenly I don't love your bialys after all these years?"

"I know you like to eat them."

"You hafta buy them if you wanna eat 'em."

"I never thought of it like that," said Yudel with a nervous raise of the eyebrows.

"That's why I'm rich and you're not. But I can change that."

"How?"

"I will give you three thousand for the recipe and another grand for everything in the store, including the ovens."

Yudel was silent for a few moments. He said, "I have other offers, you know. Let me think them over. I also have to speak to my wife."

"Let me know what other *ruhkes* offer," said the Chazzer.

"Will you match them?"

"I do not compete against ghosts. And I will not compete against myself. So you better not be making up these ruhkes because I'll take back my offer. So speak to your wife and your ruhkes. But don't speak to your idiot son. And do not think too long."

Yudel's mind began to race. That was too easy. The Chazzer was not called the Chazzer for nothing. The average person only made three grand a year. Why would he give me so much money? What if he wants to use freezing techniques and sell them all over the City? What if he wants to start a franchise? I could pay off my debts. Get those bastards out of my life. But the Chazzer would need another Yid who knows bialys. That bastard Chazzer isn't offering enough. Something is going on. But I can't overplay my hand. I could move to Long Island. I could be the first rich one in the family. The hell with that baby genius. I can play the ponies all the time.

A few days later, the Chazzer returned to the store, "Nu, Mister?"

"I've been thinking of your offer and, you know, I can be of big help to you," said Yudel.

"Why? You burning down the store and moving to Alaska?"

"Who knows how to make bialys better than me? I can be your right-hand man. More or less."

"I'll give five grand for everything, including the recipe, but not you."

"What do you mean? You don't want me?"

"It's not that I don't want you. It's others who don't want you."

"What others?"

"The others who don't come into your store anymore."

"I'll tell you soon."

"I won't take you, but I'll take your idiot son. I have idiot things for him to do. But that is my final offer, and it ain't going to change."

Again Yudel was wrapped up in thought. Five grand. That's a lot of fucking bialys. What's he up to? Should I just take the money and run or tell him about freezing them or the franchise business? But if I mention the franchise business, he'll do it himself. I do not need the Chazzer, I need the money. And he doesn't want me.

That night after diner, Jerry went out as usual. He spent his evenings sitting on cars with the other guys from the neighborhood who he thought were his friends. People would often poke their heads out of their windows and yell at them to get off their cars. They would yell back, "My ass is too good for your car," but they would move. Some nights they would pitch pennies. Mostly, they discussed things they knew nothing about, over and over again.

"The Romans invented the bath. They invented everything. No one took baths before them."

"Somebody must've invented the bath before them."

"Yeah, who?"

Inevitably, the talk would turn to the Brooklyn Dodgers where the stats were seen as similar to the way an engine revs. They would start slowly in the spring, race during the summer, and come to an abrupt halt in the winter. They always compared the three New York center fielders, but Duke always came up short against Willie and Mickey. Their unspoken consolation was that Duke was in that conversation at all.

Although Jerry's crowd were in their mid-twenties, each night seemed to end the same. One of their mothers would stick most of her body out of a window and scream, "Larry, come upstairs now before I come down and kill you." Mothers started to scream when their boys were seven years old and just could not stop.

So as soon as Jerry left the house to join his gang, Yudel told Fern about the Chazzer.

"So, you're going to sell him everything, right?" said Fern.

"This whole thing got me thinking. Instead of selling the recipe, I think I can become a bialy mogul. I could franchise the bialys and become the Jewish Howard Johnson."

"Howard Johnson's so goyisha."

"I'm just using him as a successful example."

"You know a Jewish one?"

"I'm sure there is, but I just can't think of it right now. Besides, who knows about bialys except Jews and maybe some of their goyisha friends? We could advertise. Make them sexy. We'll get pretty girls, like they do in those car ads. But to sell bialys."

"What are the pretty girls gonna do, spread their legs on a bialy like they do on cars? Just take the money from the Chazzer, and we'll figure out something afterward."

"No. I just have to figure out where to get the money from. Maybe the Boys?"

"Well, they have been good to you so far."

"You're afraid if I become successful, I'll leave you for some young broad."

"On second thought, go and ask the Boys for money. And make sure they shake your left hand when you agree on the deal."

"It was your idea in the first place to sell the bialy recipe. And the Chazzer doesn't want me," Yudel said to Fern.

"Yeah, but at least he would give Jerry a job. Think about it. Otherwise, we would have to pay someone to take Jerry off our hands."

While Yudel dreamed and schemed, I was being raised by a woman who was basically a single mom with a half-witted, one-quarter brother in the background. She loved to sing to me. After all, I was her captive audience. Although her boogie-woogie version of "Old MacDonald" was very odd, most of her tunes were the great songs from a different era.

When Fern and Yudel sat in front in the store, I usually joined them, either in a carriage or in their arms, always wearing the appropriate amount of clothes for the weather. I was a willing shill to attract business. I was the pea in the shell game, the money card in three-card monte. That was my job, and I had to help as best I could. Few can refrain from cooing at a baby, even an ugly baby. Not that I was ugly.

5

Emergency Meeting

The loss of Yudel's fingers and its many consequences necessitated an emergency meeting on the patio. The family, of course, did not tell Yudel and Fern that it was an emergency. The patio, a thin strip of broken concrete between the back of my grandparents' house and their garage, was usually reserved for Sundays and American holidays. They never met on a Jewish Holiday, save Sukkoth. Above and around it hung electric lines, phone lines, and clotheslines, sagging with the weight of memories and underwear. An occasional shard of peeled paint would float down from one of the surrounding apartment buildings as if descending from the heavens. My mother always considered those motes an omen, but of what she never said.

A curtain of dust in the garage could be seen when the sun pierced its tiny dingy window. Because of my grandfather's blindness and because my grandmother rankled at anything invented after 1900, they had no car and the garage usually lay fallow, except now. The garage was currently rented to a Studebaker Champion. The car was so long it protruded beyond the garage door and usurped part of the patio. And it was so broad that the owner could barely maneuver it up and down the narrow alleyway that led to the street between my grandmother's semi-detached house and the next semi-attached house. But this was a temporary situation. A purchase of a new car, especially a large one, usually signaled a move to a better neighborhood in the near future.

Our family arrived and left sitting. If the world could be conquered by sitting, we would be shahs and czarinas. They gathered in thick winter coats, protecting them not only from the cold but from their asses getting poked by the frayed plastic latticework holding the folding aluminum chairs together. One wooden dining-room chair, carried down two flights of steps, rose aristocratically above the peasants. And now there was a recent addition, a single shiva box from Rose Hips's funeral.

For some reason, the family did not argue about the ills that can befall the wrong people who sit on a shiva box at the wrong time. Maybe it was too obvious. Maybe it was too cold. Nor did they blame anyone for forgetting to return the lonely box to the funeral home. An extra seat was always welcome. But anyone who has been part of a family knows that there really doesn't have to be a reason for one member to get mad at another. It's almost irrational to choose one reason over another.

Usually the chairs were arranged in a semicircle around a clogged drain, but this day they sat huddled near the tiniest of grills, hoping for a spark of heat. If you wanted to sound like you did not hate the Japanese any more, you called it a hibachi. The grill rose no more than six inches from the ground on a set of spindly legs crossed like an arthritic yogi. It held no more than five cubes of charcoal and two, maybe three, burgers. My father and Tummler tended to the grill, pretending that the burgers were actually cooking as they flipped them from raw side to raw side. A February flurry fell on the meat, which made it look like it was sprinkled with coarse salt.

"We're hungry," said Muriel, which could have been said by anyone.

"We need to buy a picnic table," was an often repeated complaint as everyone would balance their plates of food and drinks on their laps or on the tubular arms of the chairs.

"You call this a picnic?" Muriel answered. "This is no picnic."

Yudel and Fern arrived late and, as soon as they did, my father mustered all the authority he could to declare, "Today we are going to discuss the future of the boy. What have Ida and Izzy have done so far? Can Yudel and Fern take care of him? What should we do together?"

Naturally my mother and father were concerned about my physical injuries, the odd and threatening events, and the questionable childrearing techniques. Certainly they must have felt guilty that they acquiesced to my grandmother's grand plan, which in turn led to those situations. Ordinarily, this would seem like a prudent and responsible parental reaction, but these were part of my education and the very reasons for the various stewardships. Unfortunately, I was still too young to speak. But instead of asking for full-time custody, my parents cleverly tried to direct and control as many aspects of my upbringing as possible without provoking my grandmother or creating animosity among the others.

The patio, which usually was the forum for prickly comments, unexpected announcements, and pointless conversation, turned into a familial version of open school night. Behavior analyzed. Grades given. Assignments assigned. Blackboards erased. I was to be judged according to the efforts of others.

My mother dealt out pieces of paper and pencils. "Danny will ask some questions, and you will write down your answers. If the answers are secret, then people will not be so mad."

"Dream on. I'm not going to write down my thoughts."

"OK," said my mother. "We won't use pencil and paper but I'll be the recording secretary."

"This is stupid. Yudel had fingers cut off because he cannot control himself. He shouldn't have the baby anymore. Period. End of story," said Tummler.

"Let's not be hasty. At least give him a chance to defend himself and show that he is not inept."

"We should be kind to Yudel; he's disabled now."

"He didn't lose his fingers at Normandy."

Fern's coat fell open. She was wearing one of those new fashionable pointy bras under a tight sweater.

"What the hell is that?" asked my mother.

"What's what?"

"What's that? What you're wearing?"

"It's the latest," said Fern.

"The latest? In what? Floozy wear?"

"They look like the old ones but in a new package," said my mother.

"I like it. Are they comfortable in there?" asked Muriel. "To me, they look like ice cream cones."

"I hope they don't leak at the bottom," said Tummler.

"Women shouldn't look like that. It does not help our gender," said Aunt Georgia.

"And you do?"

"Things must be going pretty well at the grocery."

But Fern had bought the bra with money that my grandmother gave her from the Republican Genius Dildo Fund. It was supposed to be used for food and basics since the grocery was doing so poorly.

"I'm entitled to wear what I want to wear," said Fern.

"What do you think, Yudel?"

"They're her bosoms. What the hell am I going to do? I hardly even see them anymore, anyway."

"See, they're not fit to care for the boy."

"Why? Because she wears a pointy bra?"

"Let's be reasonable," said my father.

"Reasonable?" Tummler raised an eyebrow and snorted from the corner of his mouth.

"Let's get back to why we came here," said my father. "To discuss how we all can, as a group for once, advance the prospects of the boy."

"Why are we talking at all? I'll tell you why. Because Yudel is a sick fuck gambler," said Tummler.

"If I had two hands, I'd give you a schmekelectomy," said Yudel.

"This is what the government and business wants us to do. Fight among ourselves. They're laughing at us," said Unkle Traktor.

"Always with the Commie stuff," said Yudel.

"*Gay cocken offen yom.*"

"Stop it. We need to be serious and focused. We're here to discuss the boy's future," said my father. "First, what did he learn when we was with you, Mom?"

"He didn't learn anything. He's just a baby. He just pissed, ate, and crapped like every other kid. What did you expect him to learn?"

"He learned there is a *shikker* next door. He gets so drunk he screams that he loves his wife," said my grandfather.

"That's good. Now we're getting somewhere. What did he learn from being with Fern and Yudel?" asked my father.

"Did I tell you I almost killed a burglar?" asked my grandfather.

"Yes, many times."

"Did I tell you I heard him zipping his fly as I chased him?"

"Up or down?" asked Muriel.

"Can we get back to the subject at hand?" asked my father.

"OK. Yudel's a sick fuck gambler," Tummler said.

"The boy has learned the ABCs of the grocery business," said Fern.

"You mean whatever cash you make, you stick it in a safety deposit box so you don't pay taxes. That's a good lesson."

"And Jerry would take him on deliveries."

"What do you mean? Jerry took him on deliveries? How do you take a baby on deliveries?"

"In the basket. We would tie him in the basket and throw a *schmatta* on him if it was cold or snowing."

"You can't treat a baby like that."

"Like what?"

"It toughens him up in case the heat in the apartment doesn't work."

"OK. OK. Let's just discuss what we should all try and teach the baby. So there is continuity from family to family. What does the baby need?"

"Well, a real genius doesn't need a pencil," Muriel said.

My mother dutifully wrote it down.

"Whaddya mean, he doesn't need a pencil?"

"Geniuses are always right the first time, so they can write it in ink. So he won't need a pencil."

"What happens if he likes pencils?"

"Then he won't need an eraser. Like those miniature golf pencils."

"He will need a pencil. And an eraser, not a pen, because intellectuals can't make their minds up. Too many facts. They can't make a decision."

"So he'll need a pencil sharpener, too."

"Should I include a pen?" asked my mother, but no one replied.

"A genius needs a book shelf and a scarf. A book shelf for all his smart books and a scarf for his cold neck."

"How do you know he has a cold neck?"

"Did you ever see those movies where the geniuses from England go to those famous schools? Bainbridge and Eaten. They all wear scarves."

"Bainbridge is in the Bronx. Cousin Hattie used to live near there. God rest her soul."

"That is because they have no heat. And they all wear glasses."

"Book shelves, a scarf, and glasses," said my mother as she wrote them down.

"He doesn't need suntan oil because smart people don't go to the beach. But we should make it our business to take him to the beach."

"Not Coney Island, it can get rough down there. Brighton or Manhattan Beach. Manhattan Beach is for families."

"And he doesn't need a comb. Look at Einstein's hair."

"We've already had this conversation."

"So why can't we have it again? In fact, I'm putting it on my calendar for next Tuesday so we can discuss it again."

"Wait a second. Tummler, flip the burgers," said my father. Tummler flipped the burgers, but neither side was cooked.

"Geniuses are pale. They don't need the beach. Have you ever seen Shakespeare? He was pale."

"This is crazy," said Unkle Traktor, "We're not talking about things. We must provide for his intellectual advancement."

"Commies are pretty white also. Pinky pinkos. Get it? When was the last time you were in the sun? To celebrate the Hitler-Stalin Pact?"

"There is more to a person than his intellect. There is also his physical development, his psychological health, and his moral upbringing," my father said.

"And his political education," Aunt Georgia said.

"Screw all that," Yudel said. "Look at me. You just gotta know how to do something useful, like how to run a store or plumbing."

"We don't even know if the kid's a genius. This could be one colossal Hindenburg."

The owner of the garaged car suddenly appeared and politely asked everyone to move so he could get his car out of the garage and inch toward the street. The family groused under their breath but meekly complied by grabbing everything in sight, just to reassemble, like displaced refugees, in front of my grandparents' house.

"I think we should go home," Unkle Traktor said.

"We'll go with you," Tummler said.

"Us too," Fern said.

My parents and grandparents stood stranded behind the lumbering Studebaker listening to the other family members' trailing voices as they trundled down the block.

"We can get a knish at Mrs. Stahl's and eat it on the subway."

"I like kasha knishes."

"How can you eat that? It tastes like slimy marbles."

"Think of it as caviar for us peasants."

My father took a bite of one of his raw hamburgers, and I was left in the arms of my mother for the next year. So much for the discussion of needs.

6

My First Words

My mother wanted to undo everything that my grandparents, Yudel, Fern, and Jerry had done. Not that she knew what they had done. For days she stared at me with an acute and critical eye in the hope that I would reveal some aberrant behavior. New mothers often ask their mothers for advice, but she did not have that option. How could she ask for advice without arousing suspicion? And my behavior was not reassuring. It bothered her that I did not throw temper tantrums or display defiance, as two-year-olds are wont to do, or as the child-rearing books state. She intentionally tried to goad me into a snit, just to see if I had the proper range of emotions. She placed my food in front of me and then snatched it back. And then repeated it. I reacted more like a cat swatting a ball of yarn. Her test may have strengthened my hand-eye coordination but did not seem to satisfy her concerns.

When she gave me a crayon, I made exact loops and patterns. My mother feared that my pensive and deliberate actions were the result of a misguided early education and discipline. So she took my little hand and guided it to draw quick, ferocious, random lines. It looked like the EKG of someone on the verge of a fitful death, but my mother thought it might encourage deportment more of someone my age. I mimicked her actions while she was looking. After all, I did not want to hurt her feelings or for her to believe that something was amiss. But when she turned her head, I immediately resumed my more studied manner.

My mother kept the apartment spectacularly clean, except for the tiny alcove that was my father's domain that exploded with his experiments and ideas. She tolerated and respected the area by not straightening it up. In the confined space, my father created a wonderland of half-formed creatures, surrounded by smudge-decorated walls from his forgotten formulations.

He fancied himself an inventor, except that he invented things that had already been invented or were not needed. This was not the "build a better mousetrap" type of thing. He just did not know his creations already existed.

He worked on a No. 2½ pencil. He had only seen the omnipresent and omnipotent No. 2 pencils and thought the world needed another choice. Not only did No. 2½ pencils already exist, but they were classified by Henry David Thoreau's father, who concocted a system to grade pencils. During the postclassical period, the pencil became a euphemism for the male member. If this had been more widely known, maybe it would have changed how standardized tests are administered and my father's tinkering.

He also invented things that the world did not want, such as a movable toilet. His idea was to attach an outhouse to the back of a heavy-duty bicycle. It would be pedaled around Times Square, Wall Street, or other heavily trafficked areas where large numbers of tourists and harried New Yorkers might not have immediate access to a bathroom. My father was hopeful that if you needed a bathroom and none were available, you would stand on the street corner, raise your arm, and instead of yelling "Taxi," you would yell, "Toilet!" He conceded that there would be some odd looks at first but was convinced that, once the concept caught on, it would become as common as yelling "peanuts" at Ebbets Field. My father named this invention Toodle-Loo. He believed that a British-sounding name would add an element of class. There were some scattered drawings of bicycles in his alcove, but the only blueprint resided in his head.

When my father saw me in their home, he realized that I was his most successful experiment to date. Filled with joy, he also was consumed by a sense of responsibility. Although his earlier inventions were rooted in whimsy and caprice, he now believed that he must create something both practical and durable.

As a symbol of his dedication to his newfound persona and his latest project, my father cleared a path on his worktable baring the surface for the first time in many years. He screwed a blackboard to the wall and in the whitest of chalk wrote in block letters: Fanfare for the Common Jewish Genius. A skewed but earnest tribute to Aaron Copland. My father's muse was not music, but a combination celebratory instructional manual and tool kit.

He took the notes that my mother had jotted down at the recent rudely interrupted patio session and added a few flourishes of his own.

What a Genius Needs

Pencil sharpener
No. 2 pencils (His No. 2½ pencils were unfortunately not ready for public consumption.)
Scarves
Bookshelves
Smart books (for a shelf)
Slide rule
Advice

What a Genius Doesn't Need

Comb
Wallet
Suntan oil
Permission
Girlfriend
Teeth

Baseball bat
Church key
Advice

My father added "advice" to both lists with his own sense of irony and inserted "teeth" just to see if anyone would comment. His plan was to construct a kit of the enumerated tools needed by geniuses. They would all go into a handy-dandy carrying case, and he would sell it to geniuses everywhere. He would have a Jewish version and eventually a generic version. His kit would include a brief set of instructions but first, he needed an introduction and my father tried his hand at various versions.

- He was the best of Jews, he was the worst of Jews.

- When in the course of Jewish events...

- We hold these Jews to be self-evident. But few Jews were self-evident.

My father's lack of experience and formal training in geniuses or fanfares quickly sapped his confidence, and he set the introduction aside. He could finish it later. As he continually looked at the lists for additional inspiration, he thought about what constituted the family's contribution. Could it be that the greater the distance from actual experience, the greater the clarity about what a genius needs? Or did this need more thought?

Meanwhile, he would collect a number of the items for his kit. He pushed them and his ideas around on his table the way a kid pushes peas around the dinner plate. The ebb and flow of possibilities appeared, disappeared, and reappeared on the blackboard.

Perhaps, he thought, he should write a letter to Albert Einstein, that embodiment of Jewish geniuses. After all, Princeton was a mere fifty miles from where they lived, and it might make Einstein more accessible. He would ask him the same questions he posed on the patio with the expectation of brilliant insight. But as with his introduction, my father was intimidated by the salutation. Dear Professor? Dear Mister? Dear Herr? Dear Nobel Prize Laureate? One version of the letter that quickly went into the trash used the Brooklyn approach: Dear Al.

My father found a doctor's used black satchel for the items he had amassed. The brown leather showed through the frayed handles, but as a prototype, the bag was serviceable. He put in a scarf my grandmother had knit, a slide rule, and a pencil sharpener, but he was slowed again as he became baffled by what constituted a smart book. There were obvious choices, such as a paperback dictionary, that he could stuff into the kit. But these books were instructional, not stimulating. What about the great books? Why were they great books anyway? If he picked one over another, would that be an indication that one writer was more important or more astute than another?

He enlisted my mother for assistance. One morning, at his behest, my mother headed to the Forty-Second Street library, that imposing yet accessible repository of accumulated knowledge. She requested information about the great books, and the librarian brought her three boxes of microfilm.

Microfilm machines make a fool of everyone. In this vast den of knowledge, a silent film of humiliation began each time someone tried to thread a reel correctly. And once engaged, the film screamed past the optical viewer at a speed impossible to stop on the exact spot needed or crawled too slowly to finish that day. My mother wondered if my father had sent her because he knew she would find what was needed or because he too hated becoming a public fool. The fact that others fumbled as well offered little consolation. How, she thought, could microfilm have possibly been used by spies during World War II? Finally, my mother zeroed in on the information needed. She inserted a few coins into the maddening apparatus which spewed forth photostatic copies the way a cheap consolation prize disappoints at an arcade. Unkle Traktor said that Leon Trotsky used to do research at the library, but doubted he was any better with the microfilm machines.

That night she shared what she found with my father. They looked at the blurred copies and then at each other. "This is perfect," said my father, "No one can read this stuff. So any genius worth his salt will have to make the determination on his own."

Fortunately, both of my parents had jobs to support these interests. My mother worked part-time as the receipts lady at a local cab company. The Jewish cabbie was a fixture of New York of those years, filling the streets with the corniest of jokes or political commentary, always with a bias that transcended logic. Many conformed to the stereotype of the cigar-chomping, cap-wearing skeptic, squatting in their seats, squeezing through the traffic, honking and cursing. It was impossible to get a cab in New York on Rosh Hashanah and Yom Kippur. Some guys would lend their cabs for those days to their Italian friends, even if they didn't have a hack license.

My mother sat in a bulletproof booth with randomly drilled holes for communication and air. In the summer, they provided a little fan, which offered little relief; in the winter, an extra pair of socks. Two days a week, she counted the cash against the trip sheets of the cabbies after they returned to the garage in Brooklyn at the end of their shifts. The cabbies would pass their day's receipts to her through a sliding tray in her enclosure. There were always a few who would bend over and scream through the sliding tray because they thought they couldn't be heard. When my mother came to know the offenders, she would stuff a rag into the opening on their approach, which just made them scream louder.

But most cabbies were either polite or indifferent toward my mother. After all, since they got 45 percent of the fares and all their tips, an accurate count was important. There were, of course, the guys who thought it was incumbent on them to pass rude remarks.

My mother responded in kind, "My husband's a killer, and he gets out of prison Thursday."

And after she worked there awhile, the cabbies had a standard retort: "Wasn't he supposed to get out last week?"

My mother rarely made a mistake.

My father was terribly smart and clever but not smart and clever enough to make a lot of money. During daylight hours, he worked as a salesman/cutter in the schmatta business. Usually a shop, no matter how small, had an inside man who oversaw production and an outside man who made the sales. Both watched the financials. My father did a little of each. In the mornings, he would make sales calls. After lunch, he pulled on a raggedy apron, the pockets filled with chalk, thin wax crayons, and lint, and cut the goods, which would later be sewn into women's coats.

The metallic buzz of the cutting machine would fill the air of the small factory along with the fits and starts of the sewing machines and the clang of metal rolling racks. The old unsold coats hung overhead on high hooks like criminals from the old West. When the men lifted the huge bolts of goods, the wooden floor would bow under their feet, while the tweeds and wools would poke them through their undershirts.

On the days when my mother worked, my father would take me to the shop with him. Very progressive for the times. My presence annoyed some of the men. But Nat, a fellow who worked hard all his life just to stay even, came to accept me. If my father was not watching, he would offer me sips of beer and whisper in my ear, "If you are going to be with men, you must act like a man." The sticky beer felt good on my lips.

In the cold days of winter, they prepared summer-weight garments and, in the sweltering days of summer, winter coats. During the summers, the windows were kept open to the sounds of the city. The ceiling fan blades were so large you could almost see the air circulate, and they turned so slowly you could count the rotations.

One late afternoon, my father faced a real dilemma. The shop would not be able to fill an order for an important client. They had not made enough size eights. Sixes, tens, twelves, even a few fours. No eights. And that is when I uttered my first words: "Make the sixes, eights."

Up to that moment, I had not uttered a word. That had made everyone nervous, especially those who expected words from a genius. For my parents, even a simple *Mama* or *Dada* would have sufficed. But on that day, I said, "Make the sixes, eights."

Nat and my father stared at my lips. My father was startled that I had said something, anything. Nat could not believe I offered fraudulent, albeit helpful, advice.

I repeated, "Make the sixes, eights."

When my father understood what I meant, he said, "He doesn't know what he's saying. We can't do that."

"We have to. We have to make some sixes into eights. Some tens too," said Nat. "The garments have to go today. Otherwise, we're fucked."

My father and Nat cut the labels from some of the size six and some of the size ten coats. They then replaced the cut-out labels with size eight tags, twisting the hanging loop of the tag around the button shanks. Miraculously, in a half hour, they changed all the coats into the sizes needed to complete the shipment. They knew that some future shoppers, while trying on the mislabeled size ten coats, would be elated, thinking that they had lost weight. Others who tried a sham six would despair that they could no longer fit into their usual size eight. And a few would wonder why different sizes fit the same way. In any event, I was glad I could help my Dad, even though he was hesitant at first.

"If anyone finds out, we'll tell them it was my idea," said Nat. "We don't want any trouble with child labor laws."

"Let's not tell your mother," he said. "Whatever your next words will be, will be your first words. Got that?"

I did not say a word. Well, for a few weeks, anyway.

7

Family Curse

Jerry was critical to the scheme, but he could not be told of the plan.

One evening after work, Yudel and Fern unexpectedly appeared at my parents' door. The gifts they brought only made my parents even more apprehensive.

"We thought you might need a stroller," said Fern. "It was Jerry's, but it's still in good shape."

"That was very thoughtful," my mother said to Fern.

"Or I could convert it into a bike for Jerry if you like," my father said.

"And we have this, too." Yudel marched a large corrugated box on a hand truck into the apartment and slit it open with his pocketknife to reveal a television.

"Thank you. What do we owe you?"

"Nothing."

"Well, we must owe you something."

"Save the box for the kid."

"Thank you. What's the catch?"

"I felt a little guilty about taking Rose Hips's television. Besides, this one fell off a truck."

"Thank you."

"No problem. Just don't let too many people know you have one. Or where you got it."

"Goes without saying."

"I also got one for Traktor and Georgia and Ida and Izzy, too."

"That's nice. But what does a blind man need with a TV?"

"Just tell him it's a big radio."

"I think I might paint it," my father said.

"Why would you wanna do that?"

My father did not answer at first. Finally, he said, "I think it would look better in white."

"Nobody paints their TV. And white? Did you paint your radio?"

"Yes, he did," said my mother.

"You're gonna paint the TV to disguise the evidence, aren't you?"

But my father often painted things that did not need painting. He painted the radiator cover so many times the heat could barely seep through. He painted the toilet seat because he did not want to buy a new one, and it left a white ring around his and my mother's asses.

My parents had purchased TV snack tables on sale with the hope of getting a TV one day, so this would be their first opportunity to use them. When I toddled into the room and saw the TV, I was frightened. The screen seemed to me like a gaping wound. I took sanctuary in the corrugated box. All four adults tried to comfort me and coax me from the box. They had grown up listening to and staring at the radio, but this thing stared back.

When they plugged in the television, the screen filled with snow, a modern black-and-white version only seen on electronics, with its accompanying buzzing sound that seemed like a warning.

"You have to attach the rabbit ears antenna," said my father. This he knew from reading his *Popular Mechanics* magazines. "Maybe I can learn how to be a TV repairman and do it on the side."

"Which side?" asked Fern.

My mother, meanwhile, prepared whatever was in the refrigerator and plopped it down on the snack tables, although there was no true image on the television screen.

The family chattered about this and that until Yudel finally said, "I got a business proposition. I want to start franchising bialys, but I'm gonna need seed money."

"Bialy franchise? Who the hell would buy a bialy franchise?"

"We have to teach the world about them, that's all."

"I don't have money like that. And even if I did, I don't think I would do it. It sounds like a crazy idea."

"Wait. Do you know Chazzer Cohen from our neighborhood?"

"Am I supposed to?"

"Well, he's the richest man in the neighborhood. Everybody knows that. And he wants to buy my bialy recipe. But a *macher* like him wouldn't buy it unless there was something behind it."

"So sell it to him."

"If I sell it to him, he doesn't want me as part of the business."

"Wise man."

"I would have to sign something called a noncompete clause. It means I couldn't make bialys anymore."

"The things they think of."

"Well, do you think you can help?"

"Are you making the rounds?"

"You're the first."

"I'm not sure anyone can help."

"I don't think we can help," echoed my mother.

"You never know where bialys can lead," Fern said.

"Do you know what this Chazzer person wants to do after he buys it?"

"No, but he's smart. He wouldn't waste money unless he had a plan."

I wasn't sure whether anyone could hear me but I said, "Trick the Chazzer."

My father listened more intently than the others, especially since I had helped him with his coat shortage. For one thing, he did not want me to give unsolicited advice as a career, let alone somewhat unethical advice. But, on the other hand, my advice so far had been very useful. My mother was not sure whether to be proud or concerned and she said nothing.

"Trick the Chazzer," I repeated.

"What's the kid saying? What does he mean?"

"I'm not sure," said my father.

"I think he said, 'Trick the Chazzer,' " Fern replied.

"Yeah, but how?"

"That may not be a bad idea," said Yudel. "Maybe we could fool him into thinking there's another deal on the table."

"How are you going to do that?"

The four adults formed a most unlikely cabal, adding and subtracting ornaments and embellishments to a scheme. They looked one another in the eye and rehearsed the most important dialogue until it sounded like the truth. They repeated, poked, and amended the chronology and events. When they were all satisfied that it would work, Fern and Yudel got up to leave.

"Well, since you won't invest in the bialy franchise," Yudel said, "can I have twenty bucks for the TV?"

"We just helped you! Isn't that worth something?"

"Well, originally I was going to ask for forty, but now I asked for twenty. And, after all, there's no guarantee that this plan will work."

"How much did you pay for it?"

"Fifteen bucks."

"OK, I'll give you twelve bucks," said my father.

As soon as Fern and Yudel left, my father rummaged under the kitchen sink where he kept his paints in old mayonnaise jars with the brushes erect in turpentine. He intended to change the TV cabinet from its deep mahogany to white with a decorative gold leaf.

Fern and Yudel did not tell their son, Jerry, the strategy or that he was their dupe. A few mornings later, they huddled together in the grocery and whispered loudly, knowing that Jerry would overhear them. They mentioned two offers from unnamed people for the store and the bialy recipe. One offer was a $10,000 lie. The other, a smaller figure, was the one from the Chazzer, and they discussed it with practiced disdain. They hoped their contempt for the paltry amount would give credibility to the lie. They knew their son. When he made his rounds, Jerry would brag about the double offers to his street buddies, and the word would soon spread throughout the entire neighborhood. Of course, there were other key neighborhood yentas who would be unknowing but willing pawns in spreading the story. And for good measure, they added at the end of their whispering, "I hope Jerry doesn't find out about this and tell anyone."

They also knew that, had Jerry been told the truth, he would have proudly boasted that his parents were attempting a con.

A week later, the Chazzer sauntered into the grocery and said, "I heard that you've been offered ten grand and that you're taking that deal."

"I have to get the best deal possible. I am a different person now," Yudel said, holding up his mutilated hand.

"OK. I'll give you ten-five."

"And the three of us can work for you?"

"You know, I'm a horrible boss."

"We can hack it."

"OK, ten-five, and the three of you can work for me. But you have no say in anything. I'm the boss. *Fershtay?*"

"Fershtay. Let me speak to Fern."

Yudel motioned to Fern to join him in the walk-in refrigerator. Once inside the locker, they could see their laughs materialize in the cold. Fern and Yudel covered their mouths so the Chazzer could not hear the laughs.

"Should we ask for twelve?"

"No, we don't want to overplay our hand," Fern said.

So they lingered a few extra minutes, not wanting to appear overeager. When they reemerged, Yudel stuck out his hand. "Deal."

The Chazzer said that he would be back in a couple of weeks after his lawyers drew up the papers. He took out a wad of cash from his pocket before leaving and gave Yudel a few hundred dollars. "Here's a down payment. Don't double-cross me."

Yudel starting thinking about how he was going to spend the money. He was going to move to a big house in the suburbs, probably Long Island. Get a car. If he could swing it, a Buick, fondly known in the neighborhood as a "Jew canoe." Get Fern a fur coat and take her to places where she could wear it. He would try to convince the Chazzer to spruce up the store. He would get Jerry a new delivery bike and a clean shirt.

Lost in his dream as he crossed the street, Yudel was hit by a garbage truck. Not just any garbage truck, but a private sanitation company garbage truck. The type of truck that does not pay for its mistakes and, if anything, asks its victims for money to fix the dent they had left in the bumper. If Yudel had been more thoughtful, he would have been hit by a City garbage truck, even though it would mean that the widow, Fern, and his overage orphan son would have had to wait seven or eight years for a miniscule settlement. Yudel had never given Fern or Jerry the recipe for the bialys. Nor did they buy life insurance, put money in a savings bank or create a reliable system of accounting for the grocery.

Yudel and Fern did not belong to a *shul*, and no one remembered the name or the phone number of the rabbi who conducted Rose Hips's funeral. So the family found a new one through the funeral home. I have never seen a rabbi with a suntan, and this fellow was no exception. His grayish complexion melted into his poorly rinsed white shirt. As is their wont, the rabbi gathered information from the family and wove that into a eulogy. A tale of doing good, a funny story, and suddenly someone is buried.

The rabbi began, "We are gathered today to honor our beloved Judah and his adoring wife, Sherech, and his dutiful son, Jerome."

"Who the hell is Sherech?" Unkle Traktor asked my father in a whisper.

"It means Fern in Hebrew."

"Why didn't he just say Fern?"

"It's a funeral, he's supposed to make it sound more important than it is."

The rabbi finished with, "He will long be remembered as having fingers that smelled like cheese. *Omein.*"

"Omein," repeated the men in attendance, including those from the neighborhood. This was followed by the usual hushed conversations and exchanges of condolences. Some of Yudel's racetrack buddies sent a wreath in the shape of a horseshoe adorned with pari-mutuel tickets that were crudely shaped into the words "A Winner in Heaven." All the tickets bore scuff marks they had picked up from the floor of the local OTB.

"You killed Yudel. You shouldn't have told him to sell," Tummler said to me. I was startled by his abrupt comment, which he was obviously harboring. Wait, I thought, I'm only two. They didn't have to listen to me. But before I said anything, my father interceded and told Tummler that there was no reason for such an idiotic remark, let alone saying such a thing at a funeral.

The family was not only upset that they had lost a relative, but the diner near this cemetery was second-rate although they went any way. My father ordered his favorite nondenominational dish—deep-fried French toast made from challah dipped in eggnog. After everyone had ordered and grappled with the oversized menus, my grandmother said, "He was right on the verge of becoming rich. How come every time someone in this family is about to be successful they die?"

"Nah, that can't be true."

"Yeah, what about Aunt Pearl? Remember when she collapsed just after she got her social work diploma?"

"Yeah, they were going to make a movie about her life and *bam*, she dies right there on the stage of Carnegie Hall in the middle of that graduation ceremony."

"Can you imagine how the other people felt?"

"I wonder what happened to that diploma."

"The doctors weren't sure about the cause of death, but it was probably because she was going to be successful."

"Or what about my brother, Glenn?" asked Unkle Traktor. "After the war he snuck into Wharton. You know they had a quota against Jews." Heads nodded around the table. Even if they didn't know, they automatically accepted anything that harmed Jews. "Then he got a big job at a bank because he had a crypto-Jewish name. And then his boss asked him to go out on his yacht. Bingo. Glenn goes overboard, and they never recovered his body."

"That anti-Semite bastard probably pushed him because he didn't want a Jew ruining his yacht."

"Well, of course the family didn't like that he had become a capitalist. But he shouldn't have died that way."

"You didn't like that he became a capitalist?"

"Yeah, and don't forget Cousin Flora."

"It's not easy. We also have six thousand years of success weighing on our shoulders. All those successful Jews. Making it hard on us."

"Just our luck. Moses, Einstein, Freud—all Jews."

"Even Columbus was supposed to be Jewish."

"They make us look bad."

"How can you live up to that?"

"And they're dead, too."

"So what's the solution?"

"Don't be successful."

"Just don't tell anybody."

"Then what would be the fun of being rich?"

"It's worked so far. Except for Pearl, Glenn..."

"And Cousin Flora."

"So the family is doomed."

"He's going to change everything," my grandmother said as she pinched my cheek, which I and every kid hated.

"He's the one who killed Yudel," Tummler said.

"You gave Yudel money for his fakakta bialy franchise scheme, didn't you?" my father said.

"I might have."

"What are you going to do about the five bucks he owes you?"

"Ask for it back."

8

Heel of the Bread

"I'm dying, too," said Tummler.

We gathered on the patio about six weeks after Yudel's death. Fern, of course, appeared, but Jerry could not come. He had to mind the store, even though they had hired a neighborhood kid to help out. My grandmother prepared a full meal when she heard my father was bringing his hibachi and coals. Aunt Georgia and my mother helped my grandmother while Muriel sat outside, pretending to laze on a beach. My grandfather did what he did inside the house: listened.

Unkle Traktor tried to teach me how to pronounce Dostoevsky and Chernyshevsky. I had trouble saying them correctly but realized there might be benefits to intentional or unintentional mistakes. Officials at Ellis Island had trimmed the polysyllabic names of my grandmothers upon their arrival from Russia. As neither aspired to be a writer or revolutionary, this change probably facilitated their assimilation and minimized abuse.

"What's with the bra?" Muriel asked Fern.

From the time Fern stopped sitting shiva, she wore her bullet bra continuously, leaving case markings on her like those on a spent shell.

"And your lipstick is the color of shtup."

"Here's the twenty dollars I owed Yudel for the TV," my father said, passing the money to Fern.

"Whaddya mean you're dying?" someone said.

"I'm dying."

"You said that. Of what?"

"I don't know yet."

"You just want attention."

"No, I read it in an article."

"What article?"

"I read it in a magazine at the doctor's office."

"What year was the magazine?"

"I didn't know shit for brains was terminal."

"I'm dying, and you're making jokes."

"I'm not making jokes. I'm giving you a second opinion."

Tummler and Muriel had brought their children, Jane, a sixteen-year-old, and Skippy/Basil, eight. It was hard to know which one was the mistake. The two kids seemed like they had emerged from two different wombs. Jane emitted light and hope, while Skippy/Basil doused that same light. Jane always brought me a little gift and never spoke of me being a genius. Skippy/Basil always wanted to see how sharp my grandmother's knives were.

Muriel named her children after characters from movies she loved. She loved Tarzan and hence Jane. Everyone was grateful she liked the heroine more than the chimps. Basil came from Rathbone and the Sherlock Holmes movies. But the name, of course, became the object of derision at school, and he soon declared he was Skippy. Why Skippy was a mystery to all.

My father and his first cousin, Murray, were close as kids and had attended the same public and high schools. When Murray began to work as a tummler, he insisted people should call him that. But in the etiquette of nicknames, you are not supposed to give yourself your own nickname. At first, everyone continued to call him Murray, but finally acquiesced to Tummler under his constant nudging.

A tummler's main function is to make guests laugh and create shameless, outrageous, and overly personal chaos at Jewish hotels in the Catskill Mountains. The most important targets were those who seemed like they weren't having a good time. Management wanted and needed everyone to have fun, even if it was forced. The funnier the tummler, the better the hotel, and the better the hotel, the better the tummler. Tummlers were paid a few bucks a week plus room and board, but most important, the Catskills were a place to hone their craft.

Tummler worked a few seasons at the little-known Bubby's Bungalow Bar. Bungalows were also known as *kuchaleins* or cook-for-yourselves, a good deal for families on a budget. Bubby's was a hybrid, offering kuchaleins as well as dining-room privileges. When you added the services of a tummler, Bubby's saw itself as a grand hotel.

Bubby's swimming pool lay just inches from the road. There were a few who believed that once a car had accidentally careened off the road into the water, and it was later fished out with a pool strainer. And there was a story that the fingers of one of the guests getting out of the pool were run over by a speeding car that never slowed down or stopped. Tummler used that story to say the driver was drunk—it was a "hit and rum."

Tummler asked my father to come and work with him. "There are hot-and-cold-running girls."

One year, my father finally went with him to work as a waiter. But the ritual of watching Jews eat three meals a day, seven days a week for two months almost made him convert to any religion not concerned with food, or at least one that didn't look forward to consuming fried chicken gizzards, tongue, and *kishka*. My father never returned.

Tummler stole jokes. Unfortunately, he didn't have the sense to steal good ones. He was like an incompetent jewel thief who could not tell the difference between paste and diamonds.

"A guy killed himself in the gutter. He committed sewer-cide."

"Where do people in Florida wash their clothes? Fort Launderdale."

Bubby's could not afford a drummer for a rim shot, so Tummler would yell "Hey" at the end of each joke, the cue to laugh. On Saturday nights, if the scheduled and better-paid comic died or got a bigger offer, Tummler would fill in.

The comic tradition in the Catskills was to tell almost the entire joke in English up to the punch line. That was delivered in Yiddish, especially if it was dirty. This would drive the first generation American children insane. Tummler, however, did not speak fluent Yiddish and gave his punch lines in English, but like an American tourist shouting at a Frenchman with the rude hope that others would understand because of the volume.

During the winter, he frequented Kellogg's Cafeteria on Forty-Ninth and Seventh Avenue, a place where other comics would exchange jokes and stories. Tummler tried to store the jokes he heard there the way squirrels fill their cheeks with nuts. But the other comics knew a thief when they saw one and saved their best jokes for the days when he was not there.

To add to Tummler's discomfort, there was also a company in New York named Bungalow Bar selling ice cream from trucks. Like perverts, the trucks would park near schools during the day or patrol the streets looking for children. In turn, the kids would taunt the drivers by singing:

> *Bungalow Bar*
> *Tastes like tar*
> *The more you eat*
> *The sicker you are*

Every time Tummler spoke of the Catskills, my father would sing the ditty just to annoy him. Of course, it was childish, but that was what made it effective.

Tummler had dreams of doing something that required him to be funny. Unfortunately, he had a full-time job working for New York City at the Board of Standards and Appeals. It was an obscure agency whose main requirements were wearing a frayed and stained cardigan and resisting any reasonable ideas.

While my father toiled over his hamburgers on the hibachi, the others set up a folding card table for my grandmother's food. Everyone's favorite was her potato latkes. Her Sunday soup was greeted with trepidation. The family suspected the ingredients were whatever she swept up from the floor from Monday through Saturday and then drowned in boiling water.

My father took a break from his grilling to eat something, knowing his burgers were still days from being done. He ripped off the heel of the rye bread from the end with the little union sticker and scooped some chopped liver. Union bakers stuck a white piece of paper to the moist bread to indicate who made it, but the words were always baked off, and no one knew exactly what they said.

"I wanted that heel," Tummler said.

"Well, you didn't say nothing."

"You know I always have the heel."

"I do not keep track of what part of the bread you eat."

"Just rip off the other end."

"Don't do that!" my grandmother said. "It'll get stale from both ends."

"So you'd rather them fight?" asked my mother.

"It's better that the bread not be stale from both ends."

With his fork, Tummler tried to spear the bread out of my father's hand and left four tiny indentations around the knuckles. My father dropped the bread and picked up a plastic knife. He struck a pose as if to challenge Tummler to a duel. But Tummler ignored the feint and seized the opportunity to pick up the fallen bread with the chopped liver and gobbled the whole thing down.

"What kind of savage are you?" my father asked.

"The type that won't take your son," said Tummler in return.

As part of that day's ceremony, I was supposed to be handed over to Tummler and Muriel for my first stewardship with them.

"You have to take the kid."

"I never agreed to the rules."

Tummler was right. My grandmother never had a formal contract drawn. There weren't any negotiations. There was never a vote. Everyone was assumed to have acquiesced, if seen uniquely through the narrow slits of each individual's eyes.

"We have a constitutional crisis here," said Unkle Traktor.

"I don't care. I never agreed to nothing. I'm not taking that kid."

"See. I told you! We have a constitutional crisis."

"I don't care what anybody else does or says. I'm not taking the kid."

"Come with me," said my grandmother to Tummler, falling just short of grabbing his ear. She used the voice she used for eight-year-olds.

He did not protest, and they both trudged up the darkened stairs to my grandparents' apartment.

"Sit there," she said. Tummler obeyed. My grandmother went into her bedroom, locked the door, and took out a footstool, rummaged through the top shelf of her closet, found the box with the letters RGDF crudely written on the side, and slipped her hand under the shoes and tissue to retrieve some money.

"Here's twenty bucks. Now take the kid and shut up. And don't tell anyone I gave you this. Especially Muriel."

"Fifty," said Tummler.

"Forty."

"OK." And she repeated the steps to retrieve more money.

They crept down the dim staircase back into the light to join the others. Tummler announced, "I'll take the kid. But only for a ninety-day trial run."

"He's not a vacuum cleaner."

"Either it's ninety days or nothing."

"You sure you don't want him for more than ninety days?" said my grandmother. She was miffed and glared at Tummler. She thought she had bought at least a year's peace.

"No, ninety days. Take it or leave it." At least my grandmother averted a constitutional crisis.

"And don't forget to bring him back in the original packaging."

Fortunately, the ninety days passed quickly. Tummler was in a constant snit. Muriel treated Jane, Skippy/Basil, and me the way an old mail train hooked a bag of letters as it steamed past. If I had wings,

Skippy/Basil would have gleefully plucked them off. And Jane tried to shield me from everything.

While this short stint was a great and early test of my stoicism, I still owed a debt to the Greeks and Romans. Checks and balances in government was their idea, although I am certain that bribery was never part of the equation. At least that is what the surviving texts suggest.

9

The Last French Fry Conundrum

Unkle Traktor wanted to be blacklisted. He needed to be blacklisted. It would be the affirmation of his life's work as a labor organizer, eager protestor, pamphleteer, and counselor at Camp Kinderland, whose motto was "Summer camp with a conscience since 1923." Except he could not.

The sound of Zippo lighters opening and closing echoed in Unkle Traktor's head from the thousands and thousands of meetings he had attended, all with great sincerity and intellectual intensity. The scars from being clubbed by the police and jostled by fellow protesters were gone, but Unkle Traktor wished they remained. He had been a member of so many Trotskyist splinter groups that he never bothered to laminate his membership cards. The slightest provocation or philosophical shift wrought incommensurable anger and a new faction. At times, it seemed there were more organizations than participants. Currently, he was an alternate Central Committee member of the Socialists for True Democracy (STD).

Meanwhile, while innocents were being smeared with insinuations and lies, and the lives of other Marxists, Communists, and fellow travelers were being destroyed. Yet, Unkle Traktor remained unsullied.

Aunt Georgia did not share his obsession, and their relationship defied logic and dogma.

Unkle Traktor came from the cooperative apartment buildings in the Bronx called the Coops (like chicken coops). They were built by labor unions and Jewish organizations to provide decent housing for workers and held their board meetings in Yiddish. The adults were usually apolitical. It was their children who were the activists. The police called the Coops "Little Moscow" because social and political dissidence grew like urban kudzu.

There, in the basements, playrooms, nurseries, libraries, and meeting rooms, Unkle Traktor learned not to display emotions, except for his passion for correcting social injustice and his loyalty to his incontrovertible truths and the others who pleaded for the same incontrovertible truths. Besides honing debating and organizing skills, chain-smoking was imperative. Tilting a cigarette and your head at the proper angle conveyed a sullen thoughtfulness, perfected by Sartre and Camus.

During and after graduation from high school, Esther—Aunt Georgia's real name—worked at Ohrbach's as a salesgirl. The low wages and poor working conditions prompted a walkout, considered the first white-collar workers' strike in the United States. Aunt Georgia's beauty made her the face of the mutiny, and her picture often appeared in the newspapers. Unkle Traktor was one of the union organizers, and he approached her so that they could plan "monkey business." Not that type of monkey business, but strike tactics such as giving children balloons that read: "Don't buy at Ohrbach's" by the front door of the store, or having employees release mice in the aisles of the department store to scare customers but which, unfortunately, also frightened the employees.

Aunt Georgia became attracted to Unkle Traktor's intensity, his intellect, and single-mindedness. This was in deep contrast to her family's contentiousness based on whiskers and bread crumbs. At first, she did not realize that Trotskyists were similar to Talmudic scholars, mostly men segregated by their self-imposed dogma. Using their sacred texts, both groups decided what was best for others, and both were always embroiled in schisms that mattered little to the rest of the world. Both would argue their differences with an irrational persistence and precision. And both sects had an aversion to the outdoors, particularly the sun, which resulted in their resemblance to mole rats.

Unkle Traktor's family welcomed his unexpected and uncharacteristic courtship with Aunt Georgia. They thought she might temper his zealousness. Aunt Georgia's family was happy because Unkle Traktor filled the unwritten quota that every self-respecting New York Jewish family must have at least one radical in its fold about whom they could brag of awkward acceptance. Preferably in the same sentence. Two in the same family, however, was to be avoided, and three almost begged for a raid or an investigation.

Aunt Georgia's flaw was her beauty, too conspicuous to be an intellectual or a pertinacious heretic. And though she had been raised in a row of railroad flats with stacked beds in working-class Brooklyn, Unkle Traktor feared that his comrades would judge him shallow and might conclude that his political beliefs had been diluted by sex or some other real or imagined human need. To help deflect these fears, he encouraged Aunt Georgia to study the tenets of Marxism in a pre-Cana type of way.

Of course, her studies did not change her looks, and eventually Unkle Traktor asked Esther to change her name. Initially, she was startled by the request but agreed with two provisos: one, only she could choose her new name and two, that he do something completely contrary to his personality: work for a company that advertised in comic books. After some thought, he took a job in a factory that manufactured rubber chickens, X-ray glasses, Chinese finger traps, and other useless items. He justified this as being part of the means of production that creates amusement for the masses. As for Esther, she chose the name "Aunt Georgia," an ironic and nettlesome reference to the birthplace of Stalin and a reminder of the disastrous Molotov-Ribbentrop Pact of 1939.

To temper the selection of the name Aunt Georgia, Unkle Traktor imposed a five-year plan for love, complete with deadlines and quotas. As in history, Unkle Traktor thought, but did not say, that he could change the deadlines and quotas as necessary. Not the usual mating rituals. This resulted in repeated separations, usually before May Day when planning public events was all-consuming.

Aunt Georgia and my mother thought the true problem between them was the excruciatingly long subway ride between the Bronx and Brooklyn. The Coops, located in the Bronx, the only borough of New York City attached to the United States, are to the north, while Brighton Beach is located in the south at the instep of the City. No matter the attraction or seduction, geography can be a larger issue than religion, race, ideology, or libido. Besides the Yankees-Dodgers debate or comparing Orchard Beach with Coney Island, people even hated how the streets of the others' boroughs were named, numbered, and laid out, which may seem irrational to anyone who is not a New Yorker.

During the Ohrbach's strike, a newspaper article mentioned that Aunt Georgia had been a championship swimmer in high school, and it included a photo of her surrounded by her trophies. It noted that she was also a nifty dancer, a quality greatly admired at the time. A talent agent thought she might be perfect for an Esther Williams movie and contacted her. At that time, she was with Unkle Traktor, and the likelihood of becoming anything more than an extra, even one with a needed talent, seemed remote. But during one of their many breakups, she contacted the agent. Besides the family, there was little to keep her in New York. She had plenty of other suitors, but they were mostly shoe salesmen and aspiring accountants. Reliable drudges, she called them.

Naturally, the family was afraid that the talent agent was a sexual predator or, worse, legitimate. This precipitated an emergency family meeting where, as usual, the less they knew about a subject, the louder they argued.

"See what happens when you go Hollywood? They tried to make a nice Jewish girl like Rita Hayworth Spanish."

"Rita Hayworth is Spanish, Mom," my mother said to my grandmother.

"That's even worse," said my grandmother.

"And look what happened to Fatty Arbuckle," added Tummler, sipping a Coke.

"That was over thirty years ago," said my father.

"Well, that's how bad it was."

"I read that Maureen O'Sullivan had sex with Cheetah during the Tarzan movies."

"Sex. It's always sex with you, Fern."

"She was a sucker for apes who can flip backward," said Tummler.

"Well, if you go to Hollywood and marry a *goy*, make sure it's Clark Gable."

"Finally, some sensible advice."

Off Aunt Georgia went to Hollywood to become a star in the movies. Life for her was difficult between films. The easy part was the stories the family made up to fill up the time. Muriel was convinced she was taking up with every man and was a regular at the debauched Hollywood parties. Unkle Traktor wrote to Aunt Georgia and asked to visit. When she refused, it all but fueled the discussion of her being a lesbian, a drug addict, or the next Betty Grable.

Aunt Georgia wrote that she was to appear in an upcoming Esther Williams movie scheduled to be released at Christmas time at Radio City Music Hall. This was a perfect coincidence. Besides the departure of Tummler and Yudel to save the world in the Pacific during World War II, an occasional visit to the Catskills, and the need to go to work, the family rarely ventured from their Jewish cocoon in Brooklyn. The exception was their annual outing to see the Christmas extravaganza at Radio City. Oddly enough, this yearly event played a part in the frequent breakups of Aunt Georgia and Unkle Traktor.

Once during the early Malleable Period of their relationship, Unkle Traktor accompanied Aunt Georgia and the family to the ornate theater. Immediately upon entering the lobby, Muriel hollered, "Be sure to go to the bathroom. They're gorgeous." Unkle Traktor feared that she might have been overheard by one of his union buddies, who worked there, and that his position within the STD might be compromised if it were perceived that Aunt Georgia and the bathroom fixtures were more important than his allegiance to the group. Although once inside the bathroom, he became fascinated by the contradictions of the décor. The urinals stood at attention on facing walls, forming a gauntlet for men with immediate needs, while the anteroom was a graceful example of art deco. He kept his observations to himself, not mentioning them to anyone, including Aunt Georgia. Unkle Traktor was also appalled that the family bet on which animal would shit on the stage first during the stage show. The smart money was always on the elephants. Of course, the mess was cleaned up before the Rockettes came out for their high-kicking dance routine.

The family tried to act sophisticated and contained in anticipation of seeing the Esther Williams movie but my father polished his shoes twice and Muriel counted the tickets countless times. Getting to the theater two hours before the doors opened, they ran to choose the perfect seats and ate candy they secreted in their pockets and purses as they anxiously waited. Halfway through the film, Aunt Georgia's face finally filled the screen for the briefest moment before she gracefully, but sequentially, angled into the pool with the other swimmers. The family applauded and cheered. But when they swam in synchronization, Aunt Georgia just became another pair of feet. Overwhelmed by pride and the fear that strangers would not know who she was, my grandmother leaped to her feet and yelled out, "That's my daughter's feet! Those are her legs! See the little scar by her knee." Years later, when the movies re-ran on TV, the family still screamed when they recognized Aunt Georgia and her legs, much to the annoyance of Unkle Traktor, who considered the bare legs to be like past lovers, something he did not want to discuss or acknowledge.

After the show, the family, en masse, headed to Chinatown to eat. They all believed that the number-seven combo—egg drop soup, spare ribs, fried rice, and an egg roll—was the same at every Chinese restaurant. It made sense to them that, if the waiters didn't speak English, having the same number seven everywhere in Chinatown would make things easier. Before they paid the bill, they cracked open their fortune cookies and added 'in bed' to the end of each saying. Then they crossed the street to visit the arcade to first watch the dancing chicken, and then someone would volunteer to be humiliated by losing to the tic-tac-toe playing chicken.

When Aunt Georgia's limited money, fame, and prospects evaporated, she returned to New York. She encountered Unkle Traktor at a rally for blacklisted writers and actors, some of whom Aunt Georgia now knew or thought she knew, and their version of romance was rekindled.

They were married in a civil ceremony on the second floor of the Muni Building decorated with streaked windows and a scarred tiled floor. The family was surrounded by a dozen other brides in white dresses alongside grooms in tuxedos. Unkle Traktor, however, wore a suit bought and tailored on Orchard Street, while Aunt Georgia used her Ohrbach's employee discount for a dress, bag, and shoes.

After the ceremony, everyone rode the subway to the Bronx for a buffet lunch in one of the windowless community rooms at the Coops. The entrance to the building boldly displayed a plaster frieze of a hammer and sickle.

Inside they were greeted by a variety of former neighbors with whom they had grown up and still felt a certain kinship. The musty smell of the basement mixed with the aroma of pastrami, potato salad, mustard, and sour pickles.

"Look," Muriel said, "Traktor is with his mother. Let's see how he treats her. You know what they say: you can tell what kind of husband someone's going to be by the way he treats his mother."

"Why, do you think he shtupped his mother?" Yudel asked.

"That's disgusting. That's not what I meant."

"That's what you said. And that's what married people do. Shtup."

"Maybe that's what she deserves. What type of mother makes a Commie?"

"You're going to hell."

"Jews don't believe in hell."

"Well, you're going somewhere."

My grandmother had insisted on a band. "And if the Commies don't want to dance, they don't have to," she declared. But once the musicians began, both groups joined in dancing the *kazatsky.* Rapprochement had been tacitly achieved. One family member and a party member danced facing each other with swift and true leg kicks and then locked arms, back to back, the combined balance and strength allowing them more flamboyant and powerful thrusts. A brief flare-up occurred when the dancers differed on the proper spelling and pronunciation of *kazatsky, kazatski, kazatska.* But when the guests agreed that a wedding was its own form of a political event, they pretended to like one another. Fern sang with the band, but off to the side; intimidated by their union rules and experience, she was afraid they might not let her sing with them.

A few nights into their honeymoon, I was awarded to Unkle Traktor and Aunt Georgia. They were thrilled. I became a badge of pride for Aunt Georgia and a new brain to wash for Unkle Traktor. I was their great experiment.

Unfortunately, they were not well schooled in child-rearing. They wanted me to call my imaginary friends "Marx" and "Lenin" and use my nascent math skills to verify production figures. Over time, I would have to potty-train myself, admittedly somewhat behind for my age. Something rang hollow about praising myself for such a small accomplishment. So many missteps.

Unkle Traktor had still not abandoned his dream of being black-listed. In the evenings, some of his friends would come over to discuss the state of the world and speak of the next revolution that was never to come. And they asked themselves again and again why Marxism never really took hold in the United States. Some thought it was because it was a foreign concept with foreign names, which led to foreign revolutions, which inevitably led to dictatorships. Enemies of the United States. Enemies of capitalism.

Italian anarchists were, of course, foreigners. The objects of the Palmer Raids were foreigners. Many Americans were forgetful and fearful of their own immigrant pasts. Unkle Traktor thought the STD needed to present something less threatening, more agreeable. More American. Create a simple statement, thoughtful enough to explain the basic tenets. Emotional enough to make it appealing, short enough to keep everyone's attention while not mentioning Marxism directly. Maybe food. There are, of course, foods that speak more of being American. The hot dog, watermelon, and apple pie, but perhaps they were trite symbols.

I listened to these discussions perched atop the TV Yudel had given to Aunt Georgia and Unkle Traktor. On those evenings when company appeared, the TV would be covered with a huge decorative cloth to appear as useless as possible so their comrades wouldn't think they were engaging in bourgeois activities. Finally, one evening I said, "French fries. Who gets the last french fry?"

There was silence in the room until Unkle Traktor understood what I suggesting.

"Yes. When sharing french fries and there's one left, who gets it? It's a perfect analogy for Marxism. How do you decide who gets it? How do we divide it? Should we share it? Who needs it most? What is more American than french fries? Even though they're called french fries. We can call it 'The Last French Fry Conundrum.'"

Unkle Traktor's comrades almost became animated. Toes lifted from the floor, elbows elevated slightly from the arms of the chairs followed by the obligatory justifications, nuances, and acknowledgments of each person's contribution.

On almost every night angry disagreements filled the room they occupied. Quiet and unimportant words spoken in the past become incendiary devices of the present and long forgotten topics become impassable obstacles. Convention dictated that volume and rambling won the moment. And the overwhelming sentiment: the Martyr-

Stockholm syndrome, where the six angry and unappreciated people who do everything in an organization, and resent everyone else, believe that their ideas are worth more than other's because they show up all the time, even nights and weekends.

"Yes, french fries are an everyman's food. It even has a foreign name associated with something pleasurable."

"And it's certainly not threatening."

"I think it deviates from the standard teachings," said the oldest and palest conspirator.

"But that's precisely the point. How successful have we been? If we act like outsiders, we'll always be outsiders."

"Success should not be measured by numbers, but by how we measure ourselves."

"Here's a six-inch ruler."

"We should produce a treatise. Or, at least, a broadside," Unkle Traktor said. "We must convey the urgency and import, like Marx and Engels, but without creating a parody."

"You should use a lowercase french, so it won't seem as foreign."

"There is no lowercase French."

Even as a four-year-old, I realized there are few things as dangerous as those who act from philosophical, moral, or political rectitude. They are the ones who change the world and rarely for the better. And although I did not want to be a polemicist or an accomplice to a punishable offense, I still wanted Unkle Traktor to succeed, so I offered useful suggestions once the others left.

For weeks afterward, Unkle Traktor toyed with the wording of his broadside, and I listened as he read each version. It was clear that what was important to him was not important to others. One draft included historical references to the Incas worshipping the potato and another to Germany, where they once fed potatoes only to animals and prisoners. At another point, he incorporated Sir Walter Raleigh, who gave potatoes to Queen Elizabeth as a gift and included Mr. Potato Head to soften the tone. Not ironically, Unkle Traktor and Aunt Georgia mostly ate starchy white bland food, a reflection of their beliefs. But one night, when I accidentally knocked my meal onto his work and obscured much of the writing, he understood what was needed. Less. And with some grammatical changes, it was ready.

Who should get the last french fry?

When you share a plate of french fries, no one pays attention to who ate more.

No one pays attention to who ate the big ones. Who ate the small ones?

UNTIL THERE IS ONLY ONE FRENCH FRY LEFT.

Who should get the last french fry?

Call us.

He included the phone number of STD at the bottom, deliberately omitting the full name.

"That's all of it?" Aunt Georgia asked.

"Yes. You want some mystery. You want to lure them in so they ask questions. And we don't want to alienate them at the beginning."

"But that might save everyone some time," Aunt Georgia said.

"Someday I will write the entire treatise," Unkle Traktor said.

On Saturdays and Sundays during July and August, Unkle Traktor, Aunt Georgia, a few of their radical friends, and I distributed copies of the "The Last French Fry Conundrum" broadside at the Stillwell Avenue subway stop, the workingman's portal to Coney Island. Each weekend I looked forward to standing beneath the sign that hung over the subway stairs, a remnant of World War II that informed beachgoers, "You are not in a bombing area," and this just two blocks from the sand.

In the middle of the summer heat, with our fingers smelling of the castor oil emulsion from the mimeograph machine, we dressed in long pants and collared shirts. That July Fourth, an estimated one million people came to the beach. I was encouraged to smile as I handed out the flyers but not to say anything. Silence is much cuter in a four-year-old, and if I spoke my mind, they thought it would be a distraction.

There was little interest in any politics as people came to Coney Island to eat, drink, ogle, fight, sunbathe, and meet the opposite sex. By the end of the summer, Unkle Traktor's project was so unsuccessful that he was expelled from STD, and he lost his job at the rubber-chicken factory. I felt just awful and somewhat responsible. Unkle Traktor and Aunt Georgia were so disgusted with the machinations of politics that they reverted to Morty and Esther. Of course, I inadvertently called them different things at different times. Their lives became an odd wedding announcement where both them needed a née before their names.

On Labor Day that year, a short man with a kindly smile approached Uncle Morty and extended his hand. "I am Nathan Handwerker," he said, "and I want to thank you for goosing my business this summer."

Nathan, along with his wife Ida, founded Nathan's Famous, the much celebrated hot-dog emporium. He continued, "I am not sure what you're selling, but they're buying my french fries. One guy told me he hated Commies and De Gaulle but loved my french fries anyway."

Uncle Morty was at once humiliated and proud and managed a "Thank you."

"In a bizarre way, you remind me of me years ago," Nathan said. "When I first opened Nathan's, people thought franks were bad for your health. So I dressed men in doctors' smocks to hand out free samples. But my *meshugga* idea worked. Come with me. And bring your gang for some free franks, fries, and drinks."

Nathan offered Uncle Morty a job as a french fry cutter, and he quickly worked his way up to french fry fryer extraordinaire. If you watched the french fryers, they rarely raised their heads or looked at the customers. Somehow every french fry was perfectly crisp on the outside and tender and burning on the inside. To complete an order,

Morty and all the fryers dramatically speared each order with two-tined wooden devil's pitchforks, always two bites away from splintering in your mouth. There was no need for salt as the french fryers would wipe their brows, and the sweat sprayed where it may. Nathan's allowed Uncle Morty to hang a framed copy of "The Last French Fry Conundrum" over his fryer. He had found his life's calling.

But there were other consequences. The House Un-American Activities Committee summoned me to appear before them to be questioned about "The Last French Fry Conundrum." I, too, had to go down to Orchard Street to be fitted for a suit. Usually the first suit a Jewish boy gets is for his bar mitzvah, but not me.

When the tailor started to measure my inseam, he asked, "And where are you going, *boychik*?"

"To Washington, DC, to testify before the House Un-American Activities Committee."

"You have a funny and smart boychik here," the tailor said to Uncle Morty and Aunt Esther. They simply extended their bottom lips over the top ones and nodded.

Not really believing me, the tailor added, "Don't forget to give them a *zetz* in the crotch for me. But don't mention I told you to do it."

I wish I could say that I was questioned by Joe McCarthy himself, but it was Roy Cohn, the Jewish Nosferatu. The witness table and the congressional banquettes were separated by a large expanse of worn green carpeting. I sat on a stack of phone books so I could be level with the microphone. I was more frightened of Roy Cohn's fingernails and teeth than his words.

Roy Cohn asked in a shrill and accusatory voice, "Are you now or have you ever been a member of the Communist Party?"

"I am Marxist, Senator, not a Communist, just like my Unkle Traktor, who would appreciate being blacklisted.

"No one here today is a Senator."

"Sorry, Senator."

Bobby Kennedy leaned over and put his hand over Cohn's microphone and whispered, "He's a kid. Be gentle. You do not want to lose people's sympathy."

Cohn said, "I don't care. He's a little Commie bastard."

"Let me ask you again—are you now, or have you ever been, a member of the Communist Party?"

"No. They have an age minimum."

"Are you familiar with propaganda called, 'The Last French Fry Conundrum'?"

"Yes."

"Did you or did you not write in part or full 'The Last French Fry Conundrum'?"

"Before I answer, can I take a nap? It's late."

"Do you think this is funny, young man?"

"No sir. I was telling you my schedule."

"You did not answer my question. Did you or did you not write in part or full 'The Last French Fry Conundrum'?"

I told them that I wanted french fries and Unkle Traktor thought I was giving him advice. I could have asked for chocolate milk.

"Are you trying to be funny again?"

"No sir. Don't you like chocolate milk?"

"I'm finding you in contempt of Congress. Consider yourself blacklisted."

I wasn't sure from what I was being blacklisted, but in a last desperate attempt to help, I asked, "Can you blacklist my Unkle Traktor, too?"

"No. We have a dossier on him, and he'd enjoy that too much," said Roy Cohn.

10

Me and Lenny Bruce

Although it was the mid-1950s, my kindergarten teacher's face was a relic, still reflected the Great Depression, long, dry, and furrowed. Her hair was pulled back so tightly that it made the corners of her lips curl, like the unnatural smile of a painted puppet. Her eyes focused like a raptor, and her nose was posed for any wayward smell or odious action. That face became the face of education for me.

On the first day of school, Aunt Esther and Uncle Morty walked with me, each holding a hand, in the familiar lopsided Y formation, trying to emulate a normal family. When we arrived at the front door, I was refused entry. Aunt Esther showed the principal and the relic my birth certificate and the certifications that I had received all the proper inoculations.

"We're sorry to inform you that your son has been blacklisted," said the relic. "The House Un-American Activities Committee has informed us that your son is blacklisted from kindergarten for his participation in some insidious propaganda called 'The Last French Fry Conundrum.'"

For my contribution to that broadside, I became the youngest person ever to be blacklisted and subsequently banished from kindergarten. Until that moment we did not know the exact nature of the consequences. Uncle Morty was equal parts proud, envious, and outraged. Some of the other children were simply envious. One kid asked his mother if he too could be blacklisted, so he could be sent home. But I would be the only one sent home that day. No amount of cajoling or arguing by Aunt Esther and Uncle Morty helped.

"The child is a menace to society," said the teacher, her words proven by her disapproving face.

"He's five. He's a child."

"You should have thought of that before you poisoned his mind and forced him to help you with that propaganda of yours."

"And what propaganda do you poison the children with?" Uncle Morty asked. Not the most convincing or ingratiating rejoinder. Besides, they had committed my dossier to memory, and the principal needed just two more years for her retirement. As we walked back home with my hands at my sides, I knew it was not the teacher's fault. Either her face followed her mind or vice versa. And she was the first person I met who ate yogurt because she liked it.

Even though the High Holy Days loomed, an emergency meeting convened on the patio that evening.

"Rosh Hashanah is early this year," Muriel said to each person as they appeared on the patio. Jews like to say that Rosh Hashanah is early this year. Rosh Hashanah is late this year. But I have never seen a Jew look at his watch and say, "Rosh Hashanah is right on time this year." If there is no standard, how can there be deviations?

"Yes, Muriel, we all know Rosh Hashanah is early this year."

"The boy needs a formal education."

"Maybe he should go to a yeshiva."

"He can't be a yeshiva *bohker*," Tummler said.

"Why can't he be a yeshiva bohker?"

"What normal woman wants to shtup a man with *payess*, a yellow-white shirt, and a fur hat? I'll tell you what type of woman does. A woman with a wig who needs a special bath. That's who," Fern said.

"He's five."

"For once in my life, I'm thinking about the future, and you criticize me."

"Yeah, why are their white shirts yellow?"

They discussed sending me to Catholic School, which resulted in praise for Italians for being very Jewish; distrust of nuns as aliens and overdressed in the summer; and a disdain for Pope Pius, who did nothing for the Jews during World War II.

"Why would anyone want to be a nun?"

"She was probably married once, that's why."

"Don't they have to be virgins?"

"Please. Who's a virgin anymore?"

"I once gave a nun my seat on the subway."

"Why? Did she look like Ingrid Bergman?"

"No, she looked like Barry Fitzgerald."

"There's that Greek Orthodox school," my father said.

"How can the Greeks be orthodox?" my grandmother asked.

"It's a joke."

"Yeah, but how can the Greeks be orthodox?" my grandfather said.

"It's a joke."

"They're orthodox, not Orthodox," said my mother.

"That explains it," Aunt Esther said.

My immediate future was derailed by the discussion of how Greeks could be orthodox until Tummler said, "I know what to do. But it will take money." Tummler knew another City worker who knew another City worker who could issue an original birth certificate with a different name, not a forgery, but a fraudulent birthright with a crisp seal. Once again my grandmother had to raid the Republican/Dildo/College Fund, the irony of which was lost only on Muriel.

I needed new parents if I was to go back to school. So when the new birth certificate appeared two weeks later, I moved in with Tummler, Muriel, Jane, and Skippy/Basil as abruptly as the first time.

They lived just a few blocks from Aunt Esther, so I returned to the same school, but with a different mother and father and a different name.

Tummler and Muriel escorted me to school, each holding a hand, pretending to be a family.

"How'd we get stuck with him again?" Tummler asked.

"Because you had to act like Mr. Hotshot and tell everyone you knew someone," Muriel said.

"It's Traktor's fault and his stupid Commie ideas. Who gives a shit what happens to a french fry?"

Although I heard what Muriel and Tummler said, I thought how many kids get to go Washington, meet famous people, and buy a new suit?

This time there weren't knots of parents and kids plagued by separation anxiety waiting outside the school building but layers of high-pitched screams of children that are only heard at the beach and schoolyards. This time we sought the principal and the relic because the gorgons at the gate were engaged in the usual mundane school activities. Tummler apologized that I missed the first two weeks of school, but when asked why they had not registered me in a timely manner, Tummler became flummoxed and *fonfered* something about how I attended clown school for the summer and it ran late. Most comics hate clowns and mimes, so this lie was doubly perplexing. Muriel then jumped in, "He was sick with the measles, and we did not want to get the other children sick."

The principal and the forbidding countenance stared at me.

"Hasn't he been here before?" asked the relic.

"No, this is his first day."

"I'm sure I've seen him before. Isn't he the boy who was black-listed?"

"Blacklisted! No. What do you mean? He was at clown school with the measles."

"And with the makeup, it was hard to tell he had the measles."

I wondered how old someone had to be tell a convincing lie. I already could tell better ones.

"Are you sure? He looks so familiar."

"All five-year-olds look alike. Like old people look alike."

"And some ethnic groups," Tummler added.

"Aren't you the parents of Jane and Basil?"

"Yes, we are."

"How come they never mentioned anything about having a baby brother?"

"You know how kids can be. I mean you're a teacher," said Tummler. And I hoped Jane and Skippy/Basil had memorized my new name.

They knew it was me, but neither the New York City school system nor Washington, DC, had my fingerprints yet, and although it was just a few years since Crick and Watson's discovery, the practicality of DNA use was decades away from this precinct. The relic escorted me to class and introduced me, where the other students greeted me in a singsong voice. She in turn greeted her five-years-olds, but the way an exterminator greets mice that scurry around the edges of a room. And instead of poison, she gave us warm milk and finger painting. Being two months behind in kindergarten is like missing the first years of *Three Stooges* episodes. It's easy, unless you have difficulty with hanging up your coat or sitting on the floor.

Muriel and Tummler's apartment wasn't quite ready for my arrival. My temporary bed was an assortment of towels, blankets, and pillows under the kitchen table and I was told to pretend I was camping. I imagined living under the stars if the stars appeared like twenty years of forgetting to clean the underside of a table.

The apartment was a tribute to comedy, adorned with autographed pictures of comics, ticket stubs, and notes on napkins. There were some from well-known people, including a signed picture of Zeppo Marx. "To Tummler—we have nothing in common." But most of the memorabilia was from obscure people who Tummler hoped would become famous and turn his crap into gold.

Jane and Skippy/Basil each had small rooms that reflected who they were. Jane's room was light and airy and filled with the happiest of books, except those assigned for school. Skippy/Basil's was dimly lit with pictures of guns and knives; even though they were forbidden, it was clear something lethal was secreted somewhere.

The second day of class did not go much better. There were numerous things they wanted to teach us, including how to follow orders, be quiet when told, and how to water plants. The last, I imagine, was the residue of World War II victory gardens. I told her finger painting was an odd activity; she told me to do it anyway. I did not realize until college that there was a psychological condition called *scatolia* that closely resembled finger painting. When I told her I did not like warm milk and that I could not pretend to be tired in order to take a nap, I was sent home. I did give it two days.

One night, Tummler announced that he was taking Skippy/Basil and me into the City. Muriel questioned what educational activities occurred at night, and Tummler responded, "Music. What difference does it make? Music."

"You're not taking those boys to a strip club."

"Of course not."

We trundled down the street and onto the subway and got off at West Eighth in Greenwich Village. Someone was always holding my hand. We walked a few blocks and down a few steps where Tummler knocked on a door and murmured to the bouncer, "Buddy Hackett sent me," to the guy at the door.

"You don't know Buddy."

"I knew him when he was Lenny Hacker from Brooklyn."

"But what about those kids?"

"They know Buddy too."

Tummler had run into Buddy Hackett who told him that there was a comic who was a genius who used to be a roommate of his and that Tummler had to see perform. So he brought Skippy/Basil and me. As part of the ambience, the room was filled with smoke and froggy voices, and chairs and tables that seesawed.

Suddenly a voice resounded out of nowhere: "Ladies and gentlemen, Lenny Bruce."

Bruce stared at the audience and then started his bit but as if he were in the middle of a conversation with someone else. "If you can take a hot-lead enema, then you can cast the first stone. A lot of people say to me, 'Why did you kill Christ?' I dunno. It was one those parties; got out of hand, you know. And by the way, if Jesus had been killed twenty years ago, Catholic schoolchildren would be wearing little electric chairs around their necks instead of crosses."

I didn't understand all his jokes, but people were howling. And then he started cursing, and people were laughing even louder. Before this moment people got in trouble for cursing, but he was a hero for cursing. *Fuck kindergarten*, I thought.

Then a guy at our table and four others at other tables leaped up and announced a raid. Other cops filled the room like a carbon monoxide leak. They were the Vice Squad, and this was an indecent show. We were all taken down to the station house and charged with corrupting the morals of a minor. "But if they are minors how could they be corrupting themselves?" Tummler asked.

"We have to charge them with something," said the oldest cop.

"We were just listening. Is listening a crime?" I said.

"You should have known what they were listening to," said a younger cop.

Skippy/Basil was nervous they would learn about other things, everything that he did. And now I also had a criminal record but it was the exhilarating and most confusing night in my young life.

Naturally, Muriel was furious. She was angry that Tummler did not call. She was angry that Tummler lied to her. She was angry that we went in the first place.

"What I am going to do tomorrow?" Muriel said. "It's too late to send them to school. What kind of note am I going to write? 'Please excuse my son from school today, he was arrested last night'? I married a moron."

"So did I," said Tummler.

I told the police that it was the relic who was corrupting the morals of a minor and the police said that was her job. The judge intuitively knew Tummler was not a threat to society, just to himself and his family, and that threat was well beyond his abilities. The judge told Skippy/Basil and me that he would seal our criminal indictments if we did not get into any further trouble. This was not half as troubling as the warning that my delivery cousin Jerry gave us a few days later, "You guys better watch it. Do you want to grow up and be like me?"

The police contacted the school, and within a week, I was assigned to a much younger and smiling teacher. She did, however, add her warning and said that she was going to be very strict with me because she did not want to appear to the others as a "fellow traveler" or a Commie sympathizer.

I did behave myself as she taught us how to make lopsided hearts for Valentine's Day; paper feather headdress for Thanksgiving; and for the obligatory kindergarten recital, wings for a butterfly costume, crafted from cardboard and glued to the back of an old shirt.

The only real incident for the rest of my kindergarten year was at the hands of Skippy/Basil. One of his nasty habits from the homicide trilogy of characteristics was cruelty to animals. He would capture insects and with a toenail clipper snip off their wings. When he saw my butterfly costume, he could not resist and cut my wings just as we were about to leave the house for the recital.

I had one line: "Aren't I a beautiful butterfly?" And all the parents saw was an old shirt with some stains on the back.

11

Back to Bubbe

What is more innocent than a child's preoccupation with a pail and shovel at the beach, creating an imagined world, only to be later stripped naked by his mother as she unnecessarily changes his bathing suit in front of the world to see? That world is sunbathers reposing in various shades of wan and melanoma, some staring blankly at the horizon, others lying face down with only a ratty towel separating their lips from the sand. The sun is making you dizzy by the end of afternoon.

Then there are reminders of the constant dangers.

"Don't dig that hole too deep. It'll collapse, and you'll suffocate."

Most dangers centered on drowning.

"Be careful of the undertow. It'll drag you out and you'll drown."

"The waves are too big. They'll knock you over and you'll drown."

"Don't go into the water unless there's a lifeguard. I can't save you and you'll drown."

"Just because you ate a tuna sandwich, it doesn't make you a fish. So you have to wait an hour before swimming because you'll get cramps and drown."

And all the warnings ended with "...and then you'll be sorry."

Most people do not associate beaches with New York, but there are many with their own flavors. Above the screams of children getting knocked down by the waves, only to stand up again so they could be knocked over yet again, were the shouts of vendors with skins like lizards who cried, "Hot knishes. Cold drinks." Of course they were neither. The sellers dragged their feet through the sand like the survivor in a B movie, whose plane crashed in the desert. They lugged their knishes and drinks in layers of brown shopping bags fortified by grease. The knishes were not the perfect ones from Brighton Beach Avenue. No, these were fried, baked again in the sun, and looked and tasted like third base. If the knishes remained unsold they gathered a green patina just under the crust. Everyone called the orange drinks sealed in a little wax carton *pishechtz*. When you wanted something, you yelled, "Hey, pishechtz," and the vendor would trudge over. He knew his name.

If you went to the beach early or late enough, men with homemade sieves made of a wood frame and a window screen searched through the sand for money, jewelry, and who knows what. Rumors abounded that these guys unearthed rare coins, extraordinary sums of cash, expensive watches, ingots of gold, and body parts.

One extremely hot afternoon, I sought shelter under the striped shade of the boardwalk. My grandmother sat directly overhead, playing mah-jongg. As I dug, I found four things that looked like balloons, but when I tried to blow one up, the voice of a woman, a mother no doubt, filled the beach. "Stop that boy!" The shrieking woman then added with dramatic flair, "He's going to die! He's blowing up a Coney Island Whitefish." How was I supposed to know at my age what the residue of nocturnal activities under the boardwalk looked like?

My grandmother peered through the slats of the boardwalk and was so shocked she did not finish her mah-jongg hand. She hustled me into a cab, and we raced to the hospital. Needless to say, it was my first taxi ride. The cab driver smoked a smoldering cigar, the ashes blunted by years of experience and the front windshield, and in the five minutes it took to arrive at the emergency room, the cab driver not only told us the last four hundred years of his family's history but what he planned to eat for lunch, and why it was the cheapest and best meal in the neighborhood. It was a high standard for all future cab rides.

We raced to Coney Island Hospital, a building that rose dark and dreary, even when the sun shone brightly; you half expected a beautiful but terrified young woman to scream from the top of the tower not to enter. Inside, each corridor led to another one narrower and more foreboding; the walls were painted two different colors and separated by a stripe painted by a drunk. The waiting room was cramped with patients and their families and a sign over the entrance: "Abandon all hope, ye who need hope immediately." A man rested his chin on his chest, his right arm handcuffed to the chair. Yet this was the hospital we knew.

Every one of my parents and stewards were either in attendance at the hospital or on the way. By the time the final phone call had been placed, the story became a perversion of a perversion. No one intentionally lied. They misunderstood for the sake of heightened drama.

"He swallowed a Coney Island whitefish. He's going to be a *faygeleh,*" Muriel said.

"Is that your medical opinion?" asked my father.

"As for you, Mr. You Know Everything, you watch. This'll make him a faygeleh, and then you'll know what for."

A sincere young doctor waded through the other unfortunates and approached the family. "So what exactly happened?"

"She was playing mah-jongg and left the boy alone," said Muriel.

"Is that a medical condition?" the doctor asked.

"She ruined his life."

"Shut your teeth," my grandmother said.

"For the purposes of a proper diagnosis, what actually happened?"

Everyone was quiet for a few seconds until I said, "I tried to blow up some balloons."

"Where did you find these balloons?"

"Under the boardwalk."

"Did you bring one with you?"

"What kind of sick doctor are you?" asked Muriel.

"Tummler, can you take Muriel outside?" my mother said.

"Usually an adult can accompany a child, but I think we will make an exception. Nurse, please escort this boy to examining room three."

A whopping old nurse dressed in her whites—who, just like the iceberg that sank the Titanic, was bigger below the surface—grabbed my hand and dragged me down the hall. They administered all sorts of tests and X-rays, and when I reappeared a few hours later, the doctor said, "He did not swallow anything, but we gave him some penicillin as a precaution."

"Don't they give penicillin for syphilis? He's five years old, and he has syphilis," said Muriel, who had returned by slipping past familial security.

"Madam, I can assure you he doesn't have syphilis. Just watch him for the next few days to make sure he has no adverse effects from the injection and that he didn't ingest anything that could make him sick."

"Adverse effects?"

"Yes, like swelling at the site of the injection or diarrhea."

" 'Adverse effects' is code for faygeleh," Muriel whispered aloud.

"Thank you, doctor," my mother said. "What is your name?"

"Dr. Reggiano."

"Well, thank you, Dr. Reggiano," said Uncle Morty dressed in his whites from the fry station at Nathan's within walking distance of the hospital.

"Don't say it, Muriel," my mother said.

"This is Brooklyn. Don't you have Jewish doctors?" asked Muriel.

"The smart Jewish ones are at the good hospitals. You got me," said Dr. Reggiano with equanimity.

The older people get, the less likely they are to change their house. Why spend money, if you are going to die? My grandparents were no exception. The Formica and aluminum tubing dinner table still defied gravity by standing. The accompanying chairs had a few more cuts and bruises, but the cushion stuffing had not yet escaped. And the gash in the flocking that my grandfather made chasing the intruder remained unrepaired. My grandfather sat and listened to his closest companion, an old cathedral-shaped radio. He preferred what he called "the City station."

My grandmother arose from a mythical place where she hid under the skirt of my great-grandmother. Cossacks on horseback came riding into small towns ready to kill my grandmother with a sword. The floor of the shack, dirt. This made no sense to me, but I believed every word.

My grandmother heeded the doctor's advice and did not let me out of the house for a week, and her idea of entertaining me was to retell *bubbe meises*. She had a curious manner of speaking, which made these old wives' tales even more preposterous. She spoke with a combined Brooklyn/Jewish accent (even though she came to the United States at the age of three) and delighted in words she invented. Her vocabulary included *jeet* (Did you eat?) and a favorite of mine that was not only colorful but mathematically accurate, *sums of bitches*. She sprinkled in words like *paintner, sangwitch*, and *gotkas* and added her creations like *ultatomato* (as in she gave him the *ultatomato*: either marry her or it's over), pickled herons (even though she probably never had seen a heron), bust boy (someone who cleans off tables in a restaurant), and the singer Victor Moan. I was never sure if she didn't know the real words or chose to ignore them.

Not that bubbe meises are supposed to make sense, but she told one that was particularly baffling.

"Never leave the Bible or Talmud open. Always close the book."

"Even when you're reading it?"

"Just when you're not reading it."

"Why, bubbe?" I asked.

"I don't know why. You're just supposed to listen and tell it to your grandchildren someday."

During my brief and otherwise useless convalescence, my grandfather would find my bed and sit on the edge and say, "When you're a big boy, I'm going to take you for music lessons. Would you like that?"

"Sure," I said, not knowing exactly what he meant. "Thanks, *zayda*." And then he would return to his radio.

Because my grandmother was housebound with me for a week, the mah-jongg game came to her. Every day, just after lunch, three other women would clamber up the steps to her kitchen, where they randomly called the names of the tiles. "Two bam. Three crack." There are numerous explanations for why Jewish women are addicted to mah-jongg. What started as an exotic diversion of wealthy women seeped down to the poor, who would spend hours on end playing it in the Catskills while on vacation, an exercise in bonding and cheap entertainment. But nothing explains its lasting quality.

One afternoon, it was so hot my grandfather removed one of his sweaters, and my grandmother and her three friends took off their blouses and bras and were cooling their breasts on the table as they tossed the mah-jongg tiles around them, occasionally ricocheting off their flesh with a tiny thud. These were old Eastern Europeans and by law they had to have large breasts that—when fully clothed—could be used as a snack table. But today sweltered.

As I woke from my nap and walked toward their game, two women laughed and two shrieked as one said, "He's just a boy, he doesn't know what he is looking at." And they were right; each pair looked like an extra pair of useless hands.

My grandfather emerged from his room and asked, "What's so funny?"

"Nothing, Izzy."

"I smell *mon* cookies," he said. My grandmother often made mon cookies for "her lady friends" even in the broiling heat. As always he walked with his hands outstretched, swinging them slightly, searching for the walls and furniture until he came upon the table where the women sat and began poking their breasts.

"Izzy, get away."

"What are these?"

"Kishka," said my grandmother.

"They not feel like kishka. They feel different."

"They're my kishka, Izzy, I just brought them here to show the others," said Pearl, one of mah-jongg players.

"This one is huge," asked my grandfather.

"Pearl's just showing off."

"I love kishka, can you cut me a piece?"

"Here's some mon cookies," said my grandmother as she gathered a few and poured tea into a yahrzeit glass. My grandfather carefully poured the tea into a cereal bowl to cool and then put a sugar cube between his false teeth as he drank.

"Now *gay avek*," my grandmother said.

I often wondered if my grandfather knew what he was doing when he felt up my grandmother's friends. There was an innocence and an isolation to his blindness, but he did know the world through his other senses and rarely displayed a sense of humor. Maybe this moment of rebellion was building; maybe he wanted one moment of independence; maybe he really didn't know. Maybe it was a gesture of charity by my grandmother's friends.

I never thought I would be eager to return to school, but after the events of the summer, school was welcome. As we walked to school, I thought I saw my mother hiding behind the parked cars. I looked at my grandmother's eyes, but they did not reveal anything unusual. My grandmother had to bring my kindergarten report card as the price of admission. The cardboard report was pilot-light blue, smeared with grades for walking correctly and responding to signals promptly, and the ability to dress alone. Why didn't they just add a category: behaves like an animal. How could I not be ready for first grade?

Upon introduction, the principal asked, "Is this the boy that was blacklisted?"

"What does a six-year-old Commie look like?"

"Him."

"Why don't you go after full-grown Commies?" asked my grandmother.

For the most part, I did nothing to draw attention to myself in first grade. I avoided answering the harder questions or hitting any kid who wanted to start a fight, because who knew what my grandmother would say or do if she had to come to school if I misbehaved? Everyone who went to school at this time recalls imitating a fetus under our seats and pulling our coats over our heads in case of Soviet nuclear attack. But there was a greater purpose, according to Aunt Esther. She explained that school and elected officials had to appear to do something, even if it was useless. They had to stand together during this time of great fear, and even a facade of readiness and awareness demonstrated a unified effort to combat Communism. These feckless drills taught me a very valuable lesson, especially for work life: motion is more important than results.

The school's choice of primers probably impeded my progress. They forced Alice and Jerry on us. And Jip. "See Jip run. Run, Jip, run." Where did the name come from? In Brooklyn, and I would imagine elsewhere, *gyp* means to short change someone. Why would you name a dog after petty theft? Yet from this land of simpleton texts and ingrained fears emerged a generation of overachieving Jews.

One Saturday morning there was a knock at the door. At first I did not pay attention but then when the conversation went on a bit, I tried to listen. I could see a pompadour highlighted against the wall.

"I gave you money and told you not to return," said my grandmother.

"It's about the boy."

"What about the boy?"

"I know your family, and there are things you can't teach him that I can."

"I don't know if I want him to know those things."

"No, good things. Things he can use when he becomes a man."

"Just leave."

"Books don't teach you everything. I will teach him things not in books."

"Like what?"

"You don't worry about that. I know what a boy needs."

"I know I should not do this."

"Just this once, and someday you will thank me."

"And you promise never to return."

"Yeah, yeah."

I am still not sure why grandmother relented. The Pompadour's real name was Jimmy the Hair. As we drove in his tricked-out Chevy, Jimmy the Hair asked a lot of questions.

"Did you know your Aunt Rose Hips? Does your grandmother ever talk about me? Do you know how to play basketball? Are you the genius?"

"What's a genius?"

"Someone who knows a lot of stuff."

"No," I answered to all. I thought he wanted to ask more questions but didn't. We arrived at a schoolyard basketball court, where his buddies were already playing but stopped when we arrived. Instead of playing shirt and shirtless, they played cigarette and cigaretteless. Cigarettes dangled from the corner of their mouths of one team as they dribbled downcourt. I was mesmerized as hardly an ash fell. Half the guys wore sneakers while the other half wore black leather shoes with pointy toes and soles that skittered across the playground. Although they played tough under the boards, they never got into a fight, as somehow they understood the written and unwritten rules.

That afternoon they taught me the two-handed set shot, the pick-n-roll, and the right way to fold a slice of pizza so you can eat it and not complain when it burns the roof of your mouth. Jimmy the Hair taught me how to fold dollars bills, so you could count each single twice when paying someone. He also showed me how to look and talk tough so you didn't have to fight.

"You give them a choice. You say, 'Do you want me to pull your tongue out of your ass so you will never eat a chocolate ice cream cone again, or do you want me to play stickball with your eyes and hit 'em three sewers. It's up to you.' Threats are not supposed to make sense; in fact, the crazier they are, the better." The idea of being street-smart is knowing when and whom to fight, he told me.

I came home wearing a junior wifebeater, my hair slicked back with a tube of Brylcreme, and a pack of Camels. After tamping down the cigarettes, Jimmy the Hair said that I should open the pack from the bottom so it always looks unopened, so if someone wanted to grub a cigarette, you could tell them that you haven't opened the pack yet. I also had a small pocketknife to play mumblety-peg. Please do not be concerned, I only smoked on the way back to school after lunch and after I completed my homework. A little reward. Of course my grandmother tried to stop me, but she was not on firm ground since she smoked as well, and the residue of her red lipstick on the used butts looked like she had a horrible gum disease.

I Want to Be Dangerous

"I want to be dangerous. The poor are dangerous. The rich are dangerous. But no one is frightened of the middle class. No one is frightened of me," my father said.

His latest business failure, combined with years of simmering animosity as a result of my grandmother's public proclamation that he and my mother were ill suited to raise me properly, made my father almost angry. All their lives my parents did what they thought the world wanted them to do. They had forgotten to rebel when they were young, and later they drew their lives within the edges of a stencil. The bromide "Being good is its own reward" mocked them. They just wanted to feel and be something else than they were. And then they kept hearing about the Beats. My parents were unsure what they stood for but with good reason. This small group was renowned way beyond their numbers and intentionally did not create a manifesto or rules, which was the point of it of all.

My mother was very smart, but intelligence in a woman at that time was considered a luxury, so she studied steno and wound up at the cab company. My father was also very smart but could not translate that intelligence into a consistent income. He attended City College at a time when they rode the IRT to a school that collected more Nobel laureates than Harvard, and when they exited the train, they passed through an arch constructed from rocks excavated from the first subway line. On the trip back home, their heads tilted into their books as a sign of devotion. My father studied electrical engineering, but World War II rudely interrupted his education. He enjoyed the literature and history courses but with the pleasure of an outsider. Those classes, however, did not provide a literary or historical context for Ginsberg, Kerouac, and Burroughs, and my mother and he knew Benny Goodman. He and my mother only knew Artie Shaw and Buddy Rich, but Dizzy, Bird, and Monk remained strange. Their present course of instruction became a self-inflicted GI Bill.

My parents did not meet, as much as they oozed into each other's lives. They knew each other from a near distance but like many teenagers kept their distance. They were always in different classes, but my father went out of his way to walk up my mother's block. When my grandmother wasn't playing mah-jongg, she sat on sentinel duty, staring out her window, seemingly photographing and tagging passersby like migratory birds. She knew my father's gait and his back before she knew him. One day they placed their blankets near each other at Brighton Beach. Half-naked people either attract or repel. They stayed together from then through the winter and uninterrupted to marriage and a family. The electrical engineering faded into an immediate need to support a family.

Now back with my parents, I was surrounded by Gregory Corso, Lawrence Ferlinghetti, and Neal Cassady, among others, laid open to specific and accidental pages. Bebop records half out of their jackets lay about while the music from the empty sleeves bounced off the walls. They studied more than I did, which is not really any standard.

My mother said, "I really don't understand most of this."

But when my father replied, "Neither do I," her silence brightened by this acknowledgment. I brightened as well as I cast aside my second-grade reading material and read their books filled with words and thoughts that would be banned and scorned. That meant I had much to learn.

This, however, did not deter my parents from their quest to meet the Beats. They rationalized their failure to comprehend some of the writing of the Beats, was simply part of the mystique.

They each chose distinctive styles. My mother affected the black Parisian consignment shop look and my father the acceptable mess consisting of a beret, a huge medallion around his neck, a Mexican peasant shirt, a Peruvian vest, and an Indian sash. The problems arose from their woebegone hair and glasses. The Beats wore black glasses, even if they had perfect eyesight. My father needed his tortoiseshell glasses, a style popular at the time. In order to be hip, he carefully applied black model-airplane paint to his frames, desperately trying to smooth out the bubbles and imperfections. He knew they looked repainted but was hopeful the dim light of the coffeehouse would aid his subterfuge.

My mother's hair resembled a Persian lamb coat rather than that of the female Beats, which hung straight. Their limp hair fell more as a statement that conveyed tired worldliness than fashion. To straighten her hair she tried store-bought potions containing lye that hurt her eyes and stunk up the house. She futilely tried homemade remedies such as huge rollers and ironing. Finally my parents went to a famous beauty shop in Bed-Stuy where black women had their hair straightened. They were surprised to find more Jewish women than blacks. My mother made my father keep the car windows open on the trip home so the wind could rush through her hair. It was as perfect as it was going to get.

Even with all their efforts to emulate the Beats, their basic personalities could not bend. They did not get involved in drugs, if for no other reason than that they refused to allocate money for it in their budget. Their budget was governed by several envelopes in which they deposited money until it was needed, each identified in large block letters—RENT, UTILITIES, FOOD, CAR, and ENTERTAINMENT, but no drugs. Nor could they open their home to unknown or bedraggled strangers because they cleaned every Saturday morning and did not want to make it harder than necessary. Nor could they take unnecessary car trips; gas was expensive, and they thought that aimless wondering was aimless.

My parents and I were a perfectly odd match. They were Beats, and I was a greaser, a union of malcontents brewed from the same societal ennui and conformity but swigged differently. And I was proud of them, and I hoped they were proud of me. When we walked down the boardwalk in Coney Island, the swimmers and the hot-dog eaters parted to let us pass. My parents' practiced appearance and my DA made quite a contrast to those mostly naked beach goers. A DA is when you slicked back hair looked like a duck's ass.

Now they felt better prepared to meet the Beats, so they headed into the City to the Gaslight Café for a poetry reading. My mother and father found a small table, but no one approached them for their order. My father turned to the guy at the next table, "Do you know where a guy can get a drink around here?"

"I'm Tony. Are you homosexual?"

"No, I'm from Brooklyn."

"I got some tea, man. You interested?"

"No, I'll get something at the bar."

After another fifteen minutes my father headed to the bar. "I'll have a whiskey and some Chianti." Chianti was big in those days, as their straw-covered bottles became candleholders in Italian restaurants and many homes.

"We don't serve liquor."

"What do you serve?"

"Espresso."

"I'll have two."

My father did not tell my mother how expensive the espressos were or that the strength overwhelmed him. Another half hour passed before the poetry reading began. A man dressed in a suit rose from one of the tables and walked to the head of the class. As he spoke of dirty garbage cans (as if there are clean ones), cops in their black-and-whites, and why drugs are a worthy substitute for work, he took off his clothes. His poetry was free verse but his stripping was in iambic pentameter. His alarm about privacy was confirmed by his underwear.

People snapped their fingers in appreciation. The difference between reading poetry and hearing the inflections and viewing the theater was at once distracting and exhilarating. More poetry followed with non sequiturs deep in sexual, angry, and ironic tones. They were hooked, they thought; they were glad they put in the effort. This was everything their life wasn't. As the café grew more crowded with smoke, my father tried to remove his glasses to mop his brow, but the paint had not fully dried and they stuck to his head. He tugged at them gently but they would not come off. He, of course, did not want to pull his hair or skin, but when he finally eased them off, there was an uneven black line on each side of his head and a ring around one eye like Petey, the dog from *The Little Rascals.*

"Hey, man," said Tony. "Do you know where I can get those stripes? I really dig 'em. How much bread did that set you back?"

My father, who was a salesman most of his working life and usually had an answer for everything, hesitated for a moment when Tony added, "Sorry for interviewing your brain. You don't have to tell me. That's cool."

"I made them. They're an homage to Jackson Pollock," said my father.

"How much do you want for them?"

"How much do I want for what?"

"The glasses, man. The glasses. Unless you want to give me your head too?"

"It's art, man. Not for sale."

"I can dig that, too."

And the conversation died there; neither wanted to discuss poetry, jazz, or Jackson Pollock, as they might be exposed for not knowing enough, giving the wrong interpretation, or showing enthusiasm for the wrong thought or author. The three of them were part of the periphery of the very small, disagreeable, and unpredictable group.

"It's been good talking to you," said my father.

"Before you go, man, can I grope your old lady?"

Fortunately my mother did not even hear the offer. And in a fit of solid middle-class values, my father grabbed my mother's arm never to see another poetry reading.

"Are we cool, man?" Tony asked my father's back.

For days I could sense my parents were upset, but of course, at that time I did not know the circumstances. They still wore mostly Beat clothes, but my father would change into business attire including his Adams hat with a red feather peeking out of the band. He found another pair of glasses with a slightly outdated prescription which he wore to job interviews, and would have to suffice until he started working again. I wanted to help and show them the time they invested in the Beats and me was not wasted. I changed my hairstyle and my clothes from greaser to Beat to match my parents and thought Jimmy the Hair would understand. I wrote my version of a Beat poem for a school assignment. Of course, I did not understand what I read around the house but I was an excellent mime and thief. I walked to the front of the room, stared angrily at my classmates, and read in a defiant staccato:

> *See Alice and Jerry*
> *Alice is frigid*
> *See Alice and Jerry*
> *Jerry, who knows?*
> *See Jip run.*
> *Run you motherfucker Jip, run*
> *See that motherfucker Jip, run.*

"Thank you."

"Young man, do you know what you've done?" asked the principal, Mr. Gutman.

The police had stopped my father many times while driving, so I knew that question is always answered with a "No."

"Don't be a wisenheimer."

"I'm not a wisenheimer. I don't know what I did."

"I will ask you again. Do you know what you have done?"

"No."

"You read a poem that"—Mr. Gutman hesitated for more than a moment—"didn't rhyme. It didn't rhyme."

Marvin Gutman had been a principal since principals were invented. His wooden chair now conformed to his shape and most days he simply found his way to his desk. When people greeted him warmly, he actually thought they meant it. He parked his car on the painted first base in the schoolyard but wondered why the nicks and wounds continued to mount on his fenders and hood.

"Do you want me to write it again?" I asked. "I can make it rhyme."

"No, you had your chance. Poems are supposed to rhyme."

"Why?"

"Because that is why they are called poems."

"The poems in the books my Mommy and Daddy don't rhyme."

"Then they are not poems."

"They said they were poems."

"Well the poems at school are supposed to rhyme. You are suspended for two weeks for not rhyming. And your mother and father must come here and speak to me."

"I bought cucumber seeds this week from school."

"Doesn't matter. You're still suspended."

At that age, it was all so confusing, a child trying to understand the adult world or adult actions. You don't know what certain words mean but you know they are different because of the way they are said. I was still trying to figure out why I was punished for something I thought I did right and ignored for the thing that I really did wrong. I did not care about the suspension; at that age, it is hard to miss anything at school. I brought home the cucumber seeds from school as a peace offering. Buying seeds at school was another World War II appendage when people planted victory gardens. But living on the third floor of a four-floor walk-up with little available light was not the place to grow cucumbers. My mother had some pots and soils, and planted, watered, and tended to them as if they had a chance to live.

No matter how old you are, visiting the principal's office can be daunting, but my parents had a plan. They diligently prepared for the meeting and dressed like they were attending a bar mitzvah.

"Mr. Gutman, our son wrote free verse. It is the rage these days."

"So what do I care? Poems must rhyme," said Mr. Gutman. "You know rhyming poems such as..." Gutman affected a regal baritone.

I think that I shall never see
A poem lovely as a tree.
A tree whose hungry mouth is prest
Against the earth's sweet flowing... and whatever the last word is.

"Breast—the last word is breast, Mr. Gutman," said my father.

"Just for that your son gets an extra week of suspension and so do you."

"Our son wrote free verse, a noble American tradition with Walt Whitman, who actually stole some of it from his sister, Dorothy."

"Don't educate me, I'm a principal. I should have known a wisenheimer kid comes from wisenheimer parents."

When my parents came home, my father said to me, "You did the right thing. And remember, if you are going act crazy, do it from the beginning, so people will expect it from you. If you start later they think something is wrong."

My father was right. You can be a life-long blubbering idiot, criminal, or City employee, but if your behavior changes later in life, there is obviously a problem. Especially if you threaten to violate the norms of the society. There are, of course, acceptable ways to threaten society, such as toppling the government as some socialists and Communists advocated. But toppling the government is abstract and a pain in the ass to do, as opposed to what the Beats mocked—things found in someone's home, or at least they pretended to have in their home—music, writing, sex, and drugs.

We, my parents and I, were called before the court of the most common law, which convened on the patio. Being a member of a family is like being saddled with a permanent subpoena. Whatever you did or didn't do, you must testify whether you want to or not, and pleading the Fifth is an admission of guilt. They say you are innocent until proved guilty, but then why do they keep people in jail until they are found innocent? The patio, as mentioned earlier, is where laundry is hung out to dry.

If wars could be fought sitting down, my family would dominate most of the known and all of the unknown world. Fortunately or unfortunately, they loved to fight sitting, particularly in that confined space that seemed to become narrower and narrower as they grew older. Everyone attended who could, except Yudel, who was dead, of course, but Jerry came in Yudel's stead and sat in his seat as an inherited right. This is common among humans, to claim that a chair or spot in which they or an ancestor once sat is theirs. And if they just moved a seat in any direction, a catastrophe would befall them.

Grandmother presided. "It has come to our attention that Dan and Dot have done some really stupid things, and their son has followed in their footsteps. The kid has been suspended from school because he used curse words in a poem. And someone tried to feel up my daughter."

As always my father had done his homework. You do not start up with comedians or my father. "The official reason he was suspended was that the poem did not rhyme. And no one but her lawfully married husband touched Dot."

"And you two have been hanging out with homosexuals and drug users."

"Some of the world's most important writers and artists have been homosexuals and drug users."

"So now you're one of them?"

"He's apologizing for homosexuals. He's a homopologist, that's what he is," said Muriel.

"What's a homopologist?"

"I don't know, but it's not good."

"You've been dressing like deranged children."

"This from a man who wears his neckties like a stethoscope over his ears."

"This is all bad for the kid. He's the genius who's supposed to lead us away from this mess. Remember? And you ain't helping. You and your goody-two-shoes wife."

That is then is when my mother jumped in. "*Futz in dayn gorgel*, Muriel." (Which loosely translated means, "I fart in your throat.")

There was a prolonged silence until Uncle Morty asked, "What did you say?"

"Futz in dayn gorgel," said my mother with defiance.

"How do you spell that?" asked Uncle Morty.

"She just insulted you, and you are asking her how to spell it?"

"She didn't insult me, I just want to know how to spell it."

"S-C-H-M-U-C-K," said Muriel.

"*Sha*, this is important."

"I don't know," said my mother, "F-U-T—"

She was interrupted by Uncle Morty. "Just the word *gorgel*."

"I don't know. Gorgel, G-O-R-G-E-L, gorgel."

"What are we, in the fourth grade?"

"That's not how you spell it, it's G-O-R-G-Y-L, *gorgyl*."

"That's not how you spell it, but I am not sure how you do spell it."

"I think it is G-E-R-G-E-L."

"No one's right, and everybody's right. It's a transliteration."

"What the fuck is a transliteration?"

"I told you they were hanging out with homosexuals."

"Hey, everybody, let's get back to the reason we came today."

"That's not the word at all, it's *haltz*. The word for throat in Yiddish is haltz."

"Haltz, where the hell did you get haltz?"

"Maybe it was *halz*. That's how we said it in our family."

"Your family doesn't count."

"I don't remember if it's with a 't' or not."

"How can you have two words for throat?"

"I think it is one of those Litvaks-against-other-Jews type of things."

"We have at least two words for *schmuck*: you and your brother."

My grandmother then brought out chicken and latkes. They continued arguing as they ate, spitting their food like a salt spreader after a snowstorm. The trick was to sit behind them and make sure your feet didn't touch the floor.

And then I spoke for the only time that day. "Did you know an Arab invented the zero?"

As punishment for what I said and what they claimed my parents recently did, I was rewarded with another year with my parents. Whatever reward the others expected from my being a genius was too slow in coming.

13

Invisible Success

Again, I was suspended. I raised my hand to correct a rather innocuous but erroneous answer to a common question: "Who discovered electricity?" I pointed out that ole Ben Franklin did not discover electricity but cemented the connection between electricity and lightning. While I understand that this may be an unnecessary distinction for children my age, I thought it needed to be done. There are too many myths, legends, and half-truths that are taught to children, who are only to be bitterly disappointed later in life by the truth. For example, most children believe a starfish is a fish and peanuts are nuts. They are not, and someone must stand up for the legumes and echinodermata. Although my teacher was probably embarrassed by my nuanced reply, she blamed my permanently disfigured finger in front of the entire class as a vulgar and disrespectful display. Of course, it was not the first time I raised my hand, but it was the wrong time. Mr. Gutman, the principal, attributed my latest suspension to "arrogance based on factual accuracy." My parents didn't even bother to appear at his latest kangaroo court, so thanks to their absence I was limited to a four-week punishment.

This allowed me to spend time with my father, who was still unemployed. He could not shed certain habits that he acquired while working in the schmatta business. Upon meeting a person, including strangers, he would gently rub their collar or cuff between his thumb and index finger and proclaim, "Cotton" or "Rayon." Certain fabrics were met with his nod of approval, particularly well-made woolens. Pure synthetics were not. Or when he saw a coat, he would say in passing, "That was three seasons ago." He measured his world not in years or months but in seasons, like some ancient people.

The days my mother worked at the cab company, my father and I would food shop for her, although she never allowed us to do the laundry. Her main reason was "because." On the days my mother did not work, she would take me on shopping expeditions. It was as if we had an extended family with the Kleins, Mays, Alexanders, Abrahams, Strausses, and Fortunoffs. I was the bearer of purchases and ill tidings.

Once we went into the City, instead of shopping in downtown Brooklyn, and concluded with a visit to the Automat. The Automat was an odd and eerie attraction. A solid wall of glass panes reminded me of the snake house at the Bronx Zoo, but here waited sandwiches. You looked for what you wanted, and then you put money into the wall, coin by coin. The door would click open, and you pulled out your food as fast as possible before the door slammed on your fingers. Some people remained motionless searching for their favorites, while others bobbed and weaved up and down, left and right. At times, the entire column of selections whirred, and all you saw were white flashes of the workers' uniforms who quickly and mysteriously to replenish the food. The Automat was cheap, and the atmosphere reminded me of both Coney Island and an old-age home. Elderly people lingered, pretending to eat and not very well. Most dressed like us, but men in business suits, backs erect, drank and ate, with their hats on an empty chair next to them as companions. A brutally efficient but sullen woman quickly turned paper into nickels, while shouts and laughter from customers caromed off the marble walls. Men and women, mostly women, in hairnets, wielding their oversize spoons like scepters, ladled hot dishes onto empty plates. And in the center of the cavernous room, a grand and elaborate dolphin spewed coffee. It all made no sense to me, and that was its charm.

"Sit here," she said. She left with her small fist full of change and returned with a coffee, a soda, and two slices of apple pie not à la moded. We sat in the only free seats next to a table beset by four burly men, dangerous under other circumstances, mostly with teeth. They leaned forward while listening but punctuated their sentences with dancing eyebrows and outstretched and parallel palms, and occasionally biting their lower lips when speaking. Although I did not learn the formal name or the vitality of the Socratic method until I was twelve, at that Automat at the moment, I realized New Yorkers practiced their own variety of the Socratic method. Theirs is neither as disciplined nor as refined as the Socratic version, but it is probably more efficient and less intimidating.

"Do you remember Garbage Cans?" said one of the large intimidating men.

"Garbage Cans? Garbage Cans? Whaddya talkin' about Garbage Cans?" said another.

"You know Garbage Cans? The guy got his name because he used to eat outta garbage cans? Worked for Joey? He just got out outta Dannemora."

"So what's he doing now?"

"Washing dishes at a restaurant. Whaddya think?"

"So what do they call him now, Leftovers?"

"Gotta light?"

"How come you don't got a light?"

"Why am I supposed to have a light?"

"Well, do you have a butt?"

"Of course I got a butt. Why would I ask for a light if I didn't have a butt?"

"Well, if you have a butt, why don't you have a light?"

"I don't know why I don't have a light. You got one or not?"

"Yeah, I got one, but why should I give it to you?"

My mother always enjoyed food she did not have to prepare.

Besides inventing things that already existed, my father's other creations wavered between almost practical to barely useful. With the advent of the electric knife, what was more logical than an electric fork? My father's electric fork moved like a little jackhammer, which was excellent for tenderizing meat and at the slower speed could assist the electric knife, but when turned off it was perfect for its purpose. An electric spoon made no sense at all, and none of his numerous patents made a penny. He added an eraser to the golf pencil, which otherwise would be a pencil. In the midst of a project, he wore his tape measure the way Gary Cooper bore his tin star. And on more than one occasion, he wrote an idea on a napkin only to use that napkin to wipe his face, where upon his invention would wither into crumbs or become a smudge of grease.

One morning while I was eating my breakfast and wondering why they put animals on a box of cereal, my father said to me, "Everyone pays lip service to pursuit of happiness as stated in the Declaration of Independence, but no one knows what it means. It means to have an open heart and bestow kindness on others, not some elusive obsession with self-satisfaction and money. That's what it means." My first thought was I better not raise my hand in class on this one.

"People always brag about their car, house, neighborhood, or watch," my father continued, "It is a shorthand method of saying, 'Look at me! See how successful I am!' I'll bet you from the time man first lived in caves, someone wanted to live in a bigger cave. A better cave. A nicer cave. One with a window. Or whatever they called them back then. Did you know there are cave drawings that are more than fifteen thousand years old? See, even then people wanted to hang nice things on their walls, so they could brag about them. And I'll bet you the cavemen were the first people to say, 'What will the neighbors think?' But there are things more important than things. Like being a nice person. Or being a charitable person. Or being a good parent. So you and I are going to create a formula where people can brag about something worthwhile. They will be able to say, 'I'm a nine point three on the good-person scale, or I'm a nine point six on the good-parent scale.' We will revolutionize how people talk about one another. We will make what is important, important. Something they can be proud of, besides things you can buy. We'll call it *Invisible Success*. How does that sound?"

"Great, Dad," I said as I slurped another mouthful of animal shapes.

"But remember, the road to hell is paved with good intentions so we will have to deduct points for evil behavior, which will add some balance. But first let's make a list of things we admire in others. What do you admire?"

Of course at that age, my experience was extremely limited. "Make someone laugh and blow milk out of their nose."

I could tell by the look in my father's eye that was far from his Jeffersonian ideal.

For the next few days Dad's head levitated six inches above his worktable as he searched for the best attributes of humans. He scanned his books, taking frantic notes. He phoned people and asked what was important to them and hung up before the conversation concluded, and walked away from friends he met on the street before they finished answering the same question. He watched TV with a notepad at his side.

Then one day he grabbed a gray rag and pushed the old dust on his blackboard to the side to allow for some new dust. Soon words of honorable characteristics screamed across the blackboard. Tolerant. Faithful. Creative. The blackboard soon became cramped with words and phrases at every angle. Selflessness. Book lover. Large bladder. (It was symbolic of not needing to impose on others.) Some words bowed over others, and as the day advanced, the letters became smaller and smaller even though my father said that their size was not an indication of their importance. Quiet confidence. Charity. Went to City College. (Another symbolic phrase that meant you spent money wisely.)

He stared at his mountain of words and thought it was time to assign plus and minus ratings to each word in order to create an accurate formula. Certain traits like honesty, compassion, independence, and charity of spirit were clearly more important than others, but what about witty and nifty dancer? His kept negative ones like fussy, mean, uncharitable, unforgiving, intolerant, and murderous on a pad of lined yellow paper so they did not contaminate the good words on the black-board. He seemed content with his progress until he realized there were neutral qualities like folksy, impassive, charismatic, and deter-mined. He then began a new debate with himself. At times his lips moved. "Should I just give them a zero rating? But that demeans them." At other times he looked pained when making his choices. And when my mother said, "What's important to you is not necessarily important to others," he replied, "Then I must make it important to them."

"I know what I need," he said one afternoon. "An algorithm. I need an algorithm." He explained to me the components of an algorithm and how that would help create a better formula, but when told him I did not understand, he said, "Do not be concerned, even though most child prodigies excel at math and music as there is a logic to both."

I was not the least bit concerned.

He then added, "You know, there are different type of geniuses. There are creative geniuses like Beethoven and Picasso. Then there are the geniuses like Einstein, who take what exists and explains it in a way that others can understand and use. And then there are poly-maths, geniuses like Michelangelo and Benjamin Franklin who know all sorts of things and then their ideas crash and explode in their brains to create new and grander concepts and things. And..."

I wondered how many ideas were needed for an explosion, and did it hurt?

"...you will be a different type of genius. One who sees the world clearly. One who pushes aside the chaff, swats a path in the mist, and knows that both sides of an argument are rarely equal."

"Is that good?" I asked.

"I hope so."

"What type of genius are you, Dad?"

"I'm not a genius, but I am smart enough not to tell other people that the algorithm was discovered by an Arab."

My mother had a different attitude. Every time she heard the word algorithm, she would burst out into an imitation of that singer Ethel Merman, "Algorithm, I got music, who could ask for anything more!"

And then I would sing with her even though it wasn't until years later that I got the joke.

Not only were we fortunate that my mother still had her job at the cab company, but one night she came home with a bonus. She too lived by theories, one was the larger the livery lothario, the bigger the crook, and Sam Melnick was the biggest flirt. For weeks she tracked his trip sheets. A cabbie kept 45 percent of the fares and all the tips. The cab company got the other 55 percent. Hack drivers were required to maintain a written log of every fare, but sometimes they would not throw the flag on the meter and strike a deal with the passenger. They would negotiate a fee less than the usual recorded amount, and the cabbie would pocket it all. This usually occurred on shorter trips so it was easier to conceal. The bosses reluctantly tolerated some skimming but of course fired the bigger crooks. For weeks my mother carefully monitored Melnick's trip sheets and his live time, which is when a driver had a passenger. Melnick's live time and reported fares were substantially lower than the other drivers on the same shifts. My mother informed the boss, who put a tail on Melnick for two days, and this confirmed that he was stealing. For this my mother was given an envelope with appreciation.

And as she proudly told us the story she opened up the bonus and it was five dollars. My mother looked in the envelope with one eye to see if there was more. She held it up to the light, blew into it, and finally shook it as hard as she could. "At least Melnick won't bother me anymore."

My dad wanted to contribute money as well and got the most part-time of part-time jobs. A long New York tradition is to buy the Sunday papers on Saturday night. Bundles of papers would fly off a passing delivery truck, which rarely stopped, and someone at the newsstand had to assemble the sections. And that was my father's job. The *New York Times* formed a folded mass while the *Daily News* always had dog-eared advertising inserts peeking out. People watched to make sure all the pieces were there and then double-checked to ensure the *Times*'s magazine section and the book review were included. As the day's events passed through his fingers, my father felt that they knew what was going on before everyone else. For this he received free newspapers for the week and some cigars. Since he did not smoke he sold the cigars and continued working on *Invisible Success* until one day he decided that he'd ignored me for his project and that we should build a model boat together.

We bought a block of balsa wood, some sticks for masts, and two tiny cannons, which protected the ship from nothing in particular. He drew a blueprint and shaped the balsa wood into a hull. It was then my job to smooth the wood with fine sandpaper and blow the sawdust into the air. My father gouged tiny holes, filled them with glue and planted the masts. He gently etched (uneven) patterns here and there to resemble fine finishing details and affixed one cannon on the bow and the other on the stern. I thought it would be funny if we used an old pair of underwear for the sails to which my father promptly agreed and cut the underwear into jagged triangles and attached them to the mast with heavy thread. He varnished the boat, painted some trim, and christened it the USS *Skidmark*.

We drove to Prospect Park and rented a rowboat. I think it was Muriel who told me when I was older that I was probably conceived in a rowboat in Prospect Park. My parents could not afford a cruise, and this was the best they could do. My parents' imagination was great to have such romantic notions in a clunky rowboat rented by the hour. The oarlocks did not have pins, and amateur rowers would paw the water furiously to capture a lost oar. Unforgiving wooden planks stood for seats and at the end of the season the Parks Department employees repainted the rowboats in institutional gray and never sanded the rough edges.

My dad and I each took an oar and made our way to the center of the lake, where my father launched our model boat with a great push. Immediately it began to list. A stiff breeze swept across the lake, catching our boat and making it tilt farther until the underwear sail became soaked and unceremoniously sank the USS *Skidmark*.

I wasn't disappointed at all. I had never expected it to float.

14

Bag Boy, Bag Man

I did not mind sleeping in the dog bed. The last time I stayed with Fern I was of much smaller stature and easily crammed into the apartment. The bed, a comfortable five-inch cushion measuring forty-four inches long by thirty-four inches wide, designed for large canines of sixty to ninety pounds, was a perfect fit. Why should Fern pay for a regular bed if my stint was the usual year? And who knew how large I would be on my next turn? During my first tour with Fern and Yudel, on the nights when there was no heat, I slept with Jerry. He emitted the same stale smell of cheese as his father. Thus, the dog bed was a clever and welcome solution, as it was unused and without odor.

If Fern was watching, I would scratch my head with an agitated paw motion and pretend I was trailing my tail in a circle until finding a comfortable spot before plopping down in a curl. Not only didn't Fern laugh, she thought this was my natural behavior. She called it a child's bed, and by function she was correct, and I would not bring this up at all if were not for the events of one night and the ensuing consequences.

The Chazzer wanted to enslave Jerry and Fern. The exact provisions and the selling price of the grocery store died under the garbage truck that killed Yudel, and now the Chazzer felt free to claim ownership of the grocery and all the attendant privileges. Fern and Jerry thought they were in no position to question him. He forced Jerry to wear a flour-white uniform and a pleated toque when he made the bialys, even though the ovens were in the basement. When he came up for air, he looked like a French chef in a displaced persons camp.

Jerry did, however, still wear his old belt that hung so limp and twisted that it appeared that his fly was open. In order to please the Chazzer, Jerry tried a few basic tricks such as the expectation ruse, by telling someone he would deliver in an hour and arrive in fifteen minutes. Of course, he continued using the same stale ploy long after everyone caught on. He subscribed to a trade publication where he learned that most people know the price of milk, eggs, bread, and bananas but little else. Accordingly, he lowered his price on those items and raised them on others. After a short period many people bought bread, eggs, milk and bananas from him but fled elsewhere for what else they needed. Jerry refused to fix the creaks in the floor or replace a forgotten fluorescent bulb with the transparent excuse, "That's the way my father kept the store, so that must be the way he wanted it."

Some days I would help out at the store but always avoided the black crayon. Fern and Jerry used the black crayon to tally the groceries on a brown paper bag. Fern and Jerry both would lick the crayon before using it. It might have been my imagination, but I think the black crayon actually grew from all the watering. The elderly regulars watched from upside down to see if the numbers and sums were accurate. Fortunately I can do simple math in my head. Some customers recognized this limited skill and would test my ability by asking me to add random numbers. When I performed correctly, they gave me a treat, like I was a trained seal. I did exceedingly well in math at school until one day the teacher added letters to the equations. Why do they need an x, y, a, and b if they have all those numbers at their disposal? Including the little ones they place at the upper corner of bigger numbers? It never made sense. Do English teachers randomly add numbers in the middle of a sentence?

I also bagged groceries, pulled orders from the shelves, wiped the dust from canned goods that were rarely requested, like beets and canned sauerkraut, and turned the swollen part of the cans toward the wall. Some customers were afraid I would pack the eggs and bread under the large boxes of detergent and heavy bottles of Dr. Brown's Cel-Ray soda. I must admit I encouraged this fear, especially in the mean woman with hair growing out of a mammoth carbuncle. I pretended to put the perishables in first, and then with an epiphany of sensibility, changed the order of entry. I am not often given to nostalgia, but you do not see mammoth growths with hair sprouting out of them any longer.

At least once a day Jerry would say to me, "If it wasn't for you, we wouldn't be in this mess."

"I wasn't driving the garbage truck," I said sometimes, which also had other meanings that were, of course, lost on Jerry.

One afternoon, two detectives came to question Jerry. They dressed like the Boys but not as well tailored. The cops averaged five-ten and each possessed that unmistakable tough cop mien: the bow-legged walk, taut chin, chest out, I-gotta-gun look. There were a series of home robberies in the neighborhood, and the police deduced that the burglaries occurred while the people were on vacation, whether for a weekend or two weeks. And who knew more about the habits of their neighbors than Jerry? When customers were away, Jerry would know not to make deliveries, and when he did he would always chitchat with them about this or that. I doubt they spoke of Wittgenstein and Mozart, but of family, gossip, and immediate events such as weddings and vacations. Simple but telling details and events of other people's lives, if you were paying attention.

The police questioned him on his whereabouts on specific days at specific times. To which Jerry replied, "Every day I'm at the store from seven thirty early to nine o'clock at dark, and then I hang out with the gang."

"Most of the robberies happened after nine at night."

"The guys I hang with will tell you I was with them."

"So it's a gang that's committing the robberies."

"It's not a gang with zip guns and switchblades, it's just a bunch of guys that lean on cars and make believe they know stuff," said Jerry.

"So why did you call it a gang?"

"Do you want me call it a pack of derms like elephants? Isn't that what a bunch of elephants are called, a pack of derms?"

"What are you, a wiseass?"

"I'm not a wiseass. I'm just trying to answer your questions. Jeez."

"We have our eye on you, so don't go anywhere."

"Can I make my deliveries?"

"Aren't you too old to be riding a bike?"

"I ain't putting baseball cards in the spokes and racing up the sidewalk. I'm making a living."

"OK, don't go too far."

Cops at the grocery store were not good for business.

It is unclear what attracted the Chazzer to Fern or Fern to the Chazzer. As a child, I just assumed it was natural, but in retrospect, it was baffling. The Chazzer might have thought that Fern was fulfilling her contractual obligation. And Fern might have thought seduction would secure the future of the grocery store for her and Jerry. She entered into the relationship without knowing his real name, what he did for a living, where he lived, or if he was married and had children. There could be no valid reason, except ugly people need sex too. And this is where the dog bed comes in.

One night Fern brought the Chazzer back to her room. They did not see that I had dragged my dog bed into Fern's bedroom for Jerry had had a nightmare that a woman actually welcomed him into her home after one of his ham-handed advances. The Chazzer's black coat, which he wore even in the middle of the summer, was not a symbol of his fealty to Orthodox Judaism but his office. One pocket thick with encrypted slips of paper, haphazardly arranged in an order that perhaps made sense to him, bulged larger than the others. Another pocket held two wallets gorged with cash, dog-eared receipts, and chits. Pens with half-chewed clickers, crumpled wrappers and cardboard from his addiction to Twinkies and Mallo-Cups filled what would otherwise be empty spaces. I know this because when the Chazzer undressed that night, he threw the coat in my direction, which I also used as a blanket.

In the morning, both he and Fern were startled when they realized that I was present.

"How long have you been here?"

"Since September."

"No, I mean, were you here all night?"

"Yes, Jerry had a nightmare."

"What did you hear? What did you see?"

"Nothing. I sleep like a baby." Which was untrue, as unfulfilled instructions and recriminations followed by some animal imitations had filled the darkness.

"That is good," said the Chazzer.

"Are you sure?" asked Fern.

"Was I supposed to see something?"

"No, no," they both sang.

Men like the Chazzer are impervious to humiliation; thus, they know no apologies. But for some reason he was moved by Fern's embarrassment. One can only gather that sex for him was as elusive as a natural smile. And without a history of reparations nor a clue as to what might please a child, he did what was instinctual, what he knew best: he took me with him on his business rounds.

He hid me under his coat like a sawed-off shotgun as we went from apartment to apartment, collecting rents. It was the first of the month, but the Chazzer said, "These people can legally wait until the tenth to pay, but they don't know any better. And you're not going to tell them, right?"

"Right," I said from under his coat. He obviously did not want his tenants to see me, but I wondered how many noticed an extra pair of very small feet when they answered the door.

As we moved from doorknob to doorknob, the Chazzer knew mechanically what each person owed. He slipped the cash to me, which I threw into a brown paper bag from the grocery. Just before lunch, he knocked on a door, and Mr. Gutman, the principal of my school, answered. I heard his distinctive voice through the tattered tweed. When I tried to look through the flaps in the jacket, the coat burst open. Mr. Gutman looked down at me and up at the Chazzer and said, "I'm sorry I was harsh with the boy. It won't happen again. Give his parents my regards."

"Where's my rent?"

"Wait, I'll get it."

"I don't have all day."

The Chazzer then took me to a Jewish deli for my favorite lunch—tongue sandwich, a baked-potato knish, and a cream soda. Most kids, for that matter most adults, don't like tongue. In the same way men grab their crotch when someone else gets hit there, people cannot eat tongue without thinking of biting their own.

In the middle of each table sat a tarnished and dented silver bowl with an ornate lip, filled with pickles of various shades of green. The deeper the green, the sharper the sting. Peppercorns bobbed in the brine. Another silver bowl held health salad, which is coleslaw but with a vinegar base instead of mayo. The word health is a concession, a facade for everything else you ate. You spooned the health salad into small bowls, appropriately called monkey dishes.

In Jewish delis meat was king: corned beef, pastrami, brisket, salami, tongue, and something called rolled beef. No one knew why it was rolled, what was in the roll, or who rolled it, which may explain its loss of popularity.

To be a waiter at a deli, you had to be a union member who was at least eighty years old with a ninety-year-old grudge. They dared you to tip them. Each deli assigned one waiter to be nice, which required that he tell jokes as old as the matchbook shims under the table legs. They all had practiced responses.

"If you can't pronounce it, don't order it."

"If you want lean, drink a glass of water and eat a carrot stick."

"Don't ask me; I only work here."

While the food was soul satisfying, the deli was shrouded in an atmosphere of conflict. The air was thick with the aroma of smoked meats and humidity from the steam tables. The countermen grabbed huge slabs of meat with pitchforks the size and shape brandished by the angry mob in *Frankenstein.*

For take-out orders, the countermen balanced the meat on a slice of wax paper and tossed it onto the scale, where it landed like a fighter pilot returning to an aircraft carrier. The waiters dropped silverware on the table as if the forks and knives were diseased, and they heaved hot bowls of soup onto the table with disdain. The packaged rye that framed the sandwiches became mushier with every bite until it vanished between your fingers. Near the cashier, instead of a clear glass showcase where the light gleamed off the mounds of potato salad and pools of chopped liver, shiny mirrors mocked you for how much you ate. This was our version of fine dining, but there was nothing genteel about it.

"You own Gutman now," the Chazzer said to me.

"What do you mean?"

"He is afraid of you now, because you know me."

My sandwich tasted even better.

"You are not going to tell Fern about what we did today?" asked the Chazzer. This was half a question, half a threat.

"What should I tell her?"

"That we went to a ball game."

"OK," I said, even though the Dodgers had just moved to Los Angeles, no one from Brooklyn rooted for the Yankees, and it was December.

One afternoon, maybe a week after the dog bed incident, my grandmother came to visit, accompanied by Mrs. Tillitsky, whom I called Aunt Tillie. She was slightly taller than me with a bowl haircut like Moe from *The Three Stooges*, narrow lips, and glasses half the size of her head. I think my grandmother introduced Aunt Tillie to me due to her many concerns. Besides her well-founded fear that Fern and Jerry were dense as an overcooked meatloaf and could not contribute to my intellectual advancement, Fern also told someone who told my grandmother what happened with the Chazzer, and she was fearful that I might carry a long-term sexual scar. My disdain for schoolwork grew bolder since I didn't have to adhere to the rules at school because I had Gutman in my back pocket. They knew I borrowed books from the library on varying subjects and even returned some, but that did not seem to matter.

"Do you know why I'm here?" asked Aunt Tillie.

"Because my grandmother is afraid I'm going to be an idiot when I grow up?"

"I think that is what all grandmothers secretly fear, so they say otherwise."

"Do I show signs of being an idiot?"

"Not yet."

"I brought a guitar for you, and I will teach you some simple chords," said Aunt Tillie. "With a guitar you can stir souls and have people sing along as Pete does."

She was one of the few friends of my grandmother who played neither mah-jongg nor canasta. No one told me much about her except she was once an English teacher. Mr. Tillitsky died years ago of a cello accident, the details of which are vague as he was a professional musician but apparently not a careful one. So I invented a life for her. She'd been a guide for Stanley and Livingstone. A spy during WWII. A sniper for the Irgun. She used to sing on Broadway. And she used to be taller, but being short allowed her to go unnoticed when she needed to be.

Aunt Tillie smelled of Old Spice, a scent I thought was reserved for old men, and a smooshed tissue always peeked out of her sleeve. She maintained that turn-of-the-twentieth century sensibility that the world must be a better place starting with this moment, and she only laughed at the innocent acts of children and mild jokes and never at the misfortunes of others or insults. Aunt Tillie always listened to what others said and never had the next words on her lips, so she could immediately turn the conversation back to her or her experiences. Which she called "the narrowest of prisms."

"Do you know I was blacklisted when I was five years old?"

"That's an accomplishment."

"I also have a police record."

"You're very active."

"Do you want to see my disfigured finger?"

"No, I have seen it on other people."

"If you were an English teacher, how come you didn't bring me books?"

"Who said I was an English teacher? But I didn't bring you any books, because I didn't want to you to think that one book was more important than others."

"How come you came now?"

She wore a green-and-yellow dress and had a purse full of hard candies. Sticky, round hard candies that always stuck to the cellophane with the twisted ends that otherwise could spend years in a heavy carved glass bowl waiting to be thrown out. She made a funny chattering sound when she chewed on them rather sucking on them as intended.

"I will be flitting in and out of your life. Sometimes when you need me, others when you don't. Do you know what flitting means?"

"Maybe today, not tomorrow?"

Her smile haunted me, for she was nice for no apparent reason. For that and many other reasons, she was also the first person to frighten me. I liked and needed that.

A couple of weeks later the detectives returned and told Jerry that he was no longer a suspect as they had made an arrest. They said that they nabbed two hairdressers in the neighborhood for the burglaries. The neighborhood already knew.

During their initial visit, I'd spoken to the cops out of earshot from Jerry. "Jerry is not smart enough to connect people being away and burglary, let alone how to break in without leaving a clue, and how to fence the goods."

"Look kid, stupidity is never a good defense."

"It is in Jerry's case. Check out the barbers and the guys who do women's hair. People are comfortable there and a vacation is something people brag about."

"How do you know about this stuff?"

"I grew up in Brooklyn."

Of course, they did not want to give a kid my age credit for clearing a case. One said to me, "I still don't know where you got your information, kid, but it's suspicious, and we're going to keep an eye on you."

With that good news, Jerry stole away on his bike without a grocery in the basket. Some white, some dirty, his apron strings fluttered in the wind, harkening back to the colorful streamers on his first bike with training wheels.

15

No Good Deed

When I returned to Muriel and Tummler for my next stewardship, my former spot underneath the kitchen table was waiting for me, complete with the asymmetrical stars and formations I once drew. None of which bore any resemblance to reality.

This time, as I lay still, my hands and feet now hit the table legs and chairs. If I moved those chairs, Tummler and Muriel would bump into them in the middle of the night when the bathroom called. To prepare for bed—and more important than brushing my teeth—I swept the floor for crumbs and other debris.

Normally, as I glided from one family to another, the events changed, but the people rarely did. That sameness created stability with an element of ennui. But in this household, everyone and everything seemed spasmodic and kinetic.

Tummler paid little attention to what was going on with the family. He was in the throes of trying to plump up his long-failed comic career. He could not afford to quit his City job and work the clubs full-time. He needed his City pension, no matter how meager. His act was not hip enough for the coffeehouses and the basement joints were even more edgy. But some old buddies got him gigs for five bucks a night, opening for singers during the week at some of the smaller nightclubs in Brooklyn.

Tummler turned his civil-service existence into a comic persona, changing his name to "the Mustard Cardigan," just in case some poor soul remembered his Catskills act. He wore a droopy button-down sweater, a City worker's bulletproof vest. Its tired pockets held used snot rags and crumbs and wrinkled cellophane from cookies. Just before he would go on stage, he squirted himself with a little mustard. For him, this final touch embodied the tenured *schlub*.

"My wife drives me nuts. And then we have sex."

"My daughter is so square she ran off and joined the library."

"My son and I have a lot in common. I go to a Reform temple and he goes to reform school."

He exhumed old comedy bits from his Catskills days and noted them on tiny scraps of paper found all over the apartment. But he told one joke contrary to the Mustard Cardigan image. "Love is like a warm toilet seat. You enjoy it, but you don't know who's been there before you." Tummler called this joke 'insight humor' and thought it was more sophisticated and knowing. If he could only write a few more of these, maybe he could work the coffeehouses. But he could not get "inside the joke," as comics say, or create similar ones. So he continued to work the clubs that smelled of sour bar rags.

One night, while working a club, he added a new joke. "My Jewish family is so stupid, people think we're Italian."

That prompted the club management to take him to the back alley. "You know that joke? We're gonna have to rough you up a bit."

"Didn't you like the joke?"

"Yeah, we liked it, sure. But we gotta save face."

"Can I still tell the joke?"

"Sure, but we gotta do this each time."

"Maybe you can go easier each time?"

In what they thought a masterful stroke, the parents of PS 225's PTA elected Muriel their president. Muriel naturally regarded this as a compliment, although she actually was chosen because she was impervious to pain and reason. She seemed the perfect candidate to handle obdurate teachers, delusional parents, and the tooth-cracking icing on the cupcakes at bake sales. Although she ran unopposed, she gave a campaign/acceptance speech peppered with assorted clichés, threats, and inexplicable comments.

"I will not stand for bad teachers. My son, who I will be the first to admit is not perfect, had a teacher who was dead from the neck up. I won't mention her by name, but everyone knows who she is. She's the one who got divorced when her husband ran off with someone else. And who could blame him? I know this for a fact because my friend Frieda told me. So be careful what you say at home because little pitchers have big ears. But if you elect me, don't worry. I will not act like a big macher. Thank you. Remember little pitchers have big ears."

Her position as PTA president did facilitate my re-entry to the school. I think that year I was supposed to be a cousin from Iowa. I read a bit about Iowa, although that was really unnecessary as no one from our neighborhood had ever visited Iowa. The records from my imaginary Iowa schools, often and carelessly, got lost in the mail.

Muriel did not understand her new position, nor did anyone bother to explain its responsibilities. And it is doubtful that, if they had explained them, she would have fulfilled them. One Friday morning, Muriel appeared at the school dressed in a blue skirt, a white middy blouse that strained at the buttons, topped with a big red bow, like a car at Christmas.

"I'm going to be the first PTA president to personally present the American flag at the Friday student assembly," she told anyone who would listen.

After the children were seated and quieted, Muriel marched down the center aisle of the auditorium proudly displaying the colors, hoisted in a single strap sling. Behind her, a determined but stumbling, line of nine-year-olds carried the New York State and New York City flags accompanied by a stone-faced honor guard.

"Look sharp children," Muriel commanded.

She soared more than a foot above everyone else, her bow almost touching the ceiling, and rose even higher as the entourage clambered the stairs onto the hall's stage. In bold gold capital letters across the head of the heavy curtains, one word shined, 'Asbestos.' Another example of what we once thought provided safety.

At the monthly PTA meetings, she imposed 'Robber's Rules of Order' on the sparse gatherings. There was a formal agenda and the usual circuitous discussions, in which Muriel sided with whatever made sense to her at the moment. Among a few well-intentioned parents, murmurs of Muriel's impeachment arose. They could not understand how she was elected in the first place, but their sense of decency went for naught. They were pacifists trying to murder an assassin.

Accusations abounded that Muriel threatened my teachers, that if they did not give me straight As, they would find Skippy/Basil a student in their class. Although these allegations were never proven, it coincided with the impressment of Skippy/Basil into the Boy Scouts. No Scout loomed more sinister in their official uniform. He wore his blue shirt open to expose a few unintelligible words he had carved into his own chest.

One morning on the walk to school, Skippy/Basil wrapped his yellow neckerchief around his fist.

"What are you doing?" I asked.

"If I hit someone, this will protect my knuckles from being bruised. No evidence."

"Is that in the Boy Scout manual?"

"How'd I know? Even the brown noses don't read it."

During the annual awards ceremony Skippy/Basil received two merit badges with the vague illusion that he earned them. Both badges, airplane design and citrus fruit culture, had been discontinued years earlier. But the besieged scoutmaster found them in the bottom of his sock drawer and turned them into a formal presentation. Proud Muriel sewed them dutifully onto his uniform, a bit cockeyed, but at least not pinned. He was probably the only Boy Scout never allowed to start a fire.

Up until now, Jane wore Skippy/Basil problems like a humanitarian aid worker in a war-torn nation. The efforts were well-intentioned but fruitless. And it might have been one of the reasons she turned to Eastern religions. Jane became a Jain.

One afternoon, Jane enlisted my help to make a mandala in the sand at Coney Island. Her chants of purification attracted people who ordinarily had no interest in Buddhism. We used Popsicle sticks and our fingers to create the designs.

"It should have a discernable center."

"Like the center of a Hostess cupcake," I said.

"Something like that."

People stopped sunning themselves to ask questions and offer advice. Jane would respond, "Nothing gives more satisfaction than allowing the tide and wind to sweep away what we just created. We are all temporal and temporary and so should art."

Her new found serenity allowed her to withstand taunts from the bystanders such as "What the fuck are you talking about?"

She adopted the behavior of many Westerners who had embraced Eastern religions. She started to speak in slow measured phrases, stared into space, and responded to ordinary questions in enigmatic terms. She also toyed with changing her name and tried on Tandalea, Blossom, and Satya. She was thoughtful enough just to be a weekend vegetarian and not burden the family with her dietary restrictions on the other days.

The apartment came to smell of old borrowed and yellowed texts of the *Upanishads,* the *Tibetan Book of the Dead,* and the *Bhagavad Gita,* which Jane pored over intently. She patiently tried to explain the nature of her beliefs to me, although they were new to her, too. In the end, a full understanding eluded me. Still I was determined to be supportive.

What Jane wore frightened the family more than what she read. Even though Jane was born after Cousin Flora disappeared, Jane began to dress like Flora in long skirts that swept the ground concealing her sandals. The patterns of her skirts combined lazy horizontal brown and green stitching with knobby red vertical lines that suggested she could break into a Virginia reel or a Woody Guthrie dust-bowl tune at any moment. Now Jane claimed the fabric had been spun on replicas of ancient looms of a tribe who had mysteriously disappeared from Guatemala before the Spanish conquest.

Fearful the Jane would disappear, the family always asked her where she was going and when she would return. Jane being Jane, thought they were gentle questions of curiosity concerning her welfare.

She kept her new devotions mostly private until one night at supper, they erupted in a most unexpected way. She announced, "I want to restore the symbol of the swastika to its original Sanskrit meaning of *it is*, *well-being*, *good existence*, and *good luck*."

Everyone stopped eating midbite.

"Before the Nazis," she continued, not noticing the family's reaction, "the swastika had been a symbol of goodness for over ten thousand years, and it's considered sacred and auspicious by Hindus, Buddhists, and Jains. Even the Navajos used the symbol. And did you know there are similarities between Buddhism and our practice of *tikkun olam*, 'healing the world?' "

"Are you crazy? Tikkun olam?" said Muriel.

"That's right. And the swastika has been wrongly used. It's important to change that perception."

"What are you talking about?"

"The world must know that Hitler destroyed and perverted what is revered by many."

"Are you nuts?" said Muriel. "You're gonna get us all killed."

"Go, Jane. Man, this is nuts," said Skippy/Basil, appreciative of the physical threats.

Muriel shut the windows and pulled down the blinds. She put up a kettle of water so that the whistle would drown out her daughter's words.

"If you tell anybody what you're thinking, we'll all be killed."

"Why? I'm trying to do good."

"People will only hear Hitler. Swastika. Good. And they will think we're *kapos*. Are you crazy?"

"Well then, don't call it a swastika. Call it a gammadion cross. I learned in advertising class that if you change the name of something bad, people will forget why you changed it. And if you take the weakness and pretend it's the strength, eventually people will believe that, too."

"For this we sent you to college?"

"This will be my life's work. I must take on a task that is meaningful. It was a beautiful symbol before the Nazis destroyed it."

"Can't you hand this over to one of your strange friends?"

"It's more meaningful coming from a Jew."

"Don't you have Jewish friends as nuts as you? Let them die."

"See, I don't look so bad anymore. Right?" said Skippy/Basil turning to Muriel and me for acknowledgment.

Tummler was working a gig that night and would not be home for hours. But Muriel was tenacious and wouldn't concede a point. Even Skippy/Basil sitting across from me at the dining-room table began to understand the implications of what Jane was doing. I watched in silent horror.

"Have you told anybody else this?"

"Not yet. I'm formulating a campaign of goodness and redemption."

"Fine. Think whatever you want. But keep your trap shut. You hear me?"

Frantic, Muriel called my grandmother. When Tummler finally arrived home with fresh bruises, Muriel took him into the bathroom where we could hear their voices quivering in fear, anger, and disbelief.

A few weeks later, as Skippy/Basil and I prepared for school, we saw Tummler and Muriel emerge from their bedroom dressed as if they were attending either a wedding or a funeral. He never went to work in a suit. She wore more makeup than I thought she owned. My grandmother knocked on the door, also dressed up, pretending that all was normal.

"Do you have the money?" Muriel asked her in a whisper.

Jane emerged from her room carrying a suitcase in one hand while defiantly waving her newly minted passport in the other in anticipation of the next question. She hugged and pecked Skippy/Basil and myself silently on the cheek. The next knock on the door was Norman, the next-door neighbor and cab driver.

They headed for Idlewild Airport. Except for Norman, it was their first visit. Upon arrival at the Pan Am pavilion, my grandmother went to the ticket counter.

"Do you know where India is?" she asked.

"Yes."

"Good. Do you know how to get there?"

"Yes."

"Good. Do the planes come back?"

"Most times," said the woman in her matching airline outfit and hat.

"Good. How often do you go?"

"We go three times a week."

"How about today?"

"Yes, this afternoon."

"Good. I just wanted to make sure before I give you my money. It's for my granddaughter. She has ideas of her own, you know."

16

Wrong Train

Unkle Traktor and Aunt Georgia took me to the old Penn Station, a new-world imitation of the Baths of Caracalla and the Gare d'Orsay. Hundreds of kids bound for summer camp appeared and disappeared in the shafts of sunlight as they waved good-bye and traipsed down the platforms to their trains. I threw my duffel bag over my shoulder, grabbed my guitar case, and joined the herd. Some children cried; others never looked back. Some parents cried; others planned lunch and longer vacations. Anxiety, excitement, and unclear track assignments filled the terminal.

From the beginning, nothing on the train seemed right. Many of the girls sported bobbed noses and the boys' haircuts were measured and fashioned, not just mowed short for the hot summer. Their pastel shirts seemed far too happy and crisp. I had never heard socialists laugh so much. Even at my age, socialists were required to bear the weight of the world on our shoulders and faces, if for no other reason than to prepare us for being adults. And no one but me brought a sandwich and an apple. A salami sandwich designed to withstand hours of inattention and lack of refrigeration sat next to me identified by the spreading grease stain on the brown bag and the pungent smell of fat and spices.

As the train inched along the Hudson River, counselors called out the names of the campers. My name was nowhere to be heard. If there were any Jews in the crowd, they had crypto-Jewish names like Brown, Stone, or Rose. I continued to listen for my name. Two hours later, when we alit from the train, I approached the oldest adults. They furiously scrutinized their lists.

"Where are you supposed to be again?"

"Camp Emma Goldman. Sacco and Vanzetti Cabin. Rifton, New York. Where Sojourner Truth was born."

"You're in the wrong place. This is Camp Sunshine."

"Camp Sunshine?" I said. "Sounds like one of those the fresh-air camps."

"I can assure you that we are not a Fresh Air Fund camp," said one of the adults with the borrowed contempt of a salesperson in an expensive store. They huddled and murmured among themselves.

"What are we going to do? We never make mistakes."

"Of course not. It's the boy's fault."

"But what to do? We can't just leave him here."

"We must make lemon poppy-seed cake from lemons."

They turned to me.

"How old are you?"

"Twelve."

"Twelve. Twelve. Well, a twelve-year-old boy should be with the Noble Savages."

"But that doesn't solve the bigger problem."

"I got it. We'll make him a pet. A mascot. A project. He'll be the first Camp Sunshine Fellow."

"Excellent."

"Would you like to be the first Camp Sunshine Fellow?"

"I guess," I said.

"We'll give you three-quarter privileges."

"Does three-quarter privileges include lunch?" I asked.

"Yes."

"Every day?"

"Yes."

"OK."

"Get on that bus."

The buses were not the standard yellow buses owned by companies like Ed-Deb Trans, with hardened lumps of gum under the seats and young love carved into the seat cushions. These buses were benevolent whales with air conditioning that formed a hump on the roof and individual reading lights that glittered like eyes.

It was clear now. Not only did I get on the wrong train, but I was going to a camp for socialites, not socialists. Not a common error, and one for which I had no excuse.

When we arrived at Sunshine, I said, "I have to call my guardians."

I was led to a phone, where I called Aunt Georgia and Unkle Traktor to explain the situation. I imagined them sharing the receiver.

"How did you get on the wrong train?"

"They all looked alike."

"Are they treating you well?"

"The offered me three-quarter privileges. It's a fellowship."

"What does that mean?"

"I'm not sure. But it includes lunch."

"Do they know you're Jewish?"

"They know that I was supposed to go to Camp Emma Goldman. Sacco and Vanzetti Cabin. Rifton, New York, where Sojourner Truth was born."

"So they know you're Jewish. And that three-quarters thing means the camp is restricted. They will exclude you from what they want and hide behind that phony fellowship. Dirty bastards. Let's figure out a way to get you to the right camp."

I felt awful and stupid about the entire situation until Aunt Georgia said, "Wait. Maybe you can stay, and you can be a Margaret Mead in reverse. You can observe and verify what we suspect already, and when you return home, you can write about it."

"Yes, yes, maybe that's a better idea," Unkle Traktor said. "What an opportunity. Then when you get home, you can write 'How Those Dirty Bastards Really Live.'"

"We'll work on the title later," said Aunt Georgia. "But remember, while you're there, don't write anything down. Just take mental notes. Written notes can be used against you. Remember Alger Hiss and the Pumpkin Papers."

The more we spoke, the less guilty I felt and the more enthusiastic I became about my mistake.

"OK, stay. But be careful. Those dirty bastards," Unkle Traktor said before they hung up. Aunt Georgia then called Emma Goldman and told them that I would not be coming for lunch.

The Noble Savages cabin had only five other boys my age, and they all knew each other from previous summers: Biff; the twins, Tad and Trey; Ed; and Mellon, who bore his mother's maiden name as his first. My bunkmates tried the usual pranks—short-sheeting the beds, Saran Wrap over the toilet bowl, and passing off Ex-Lax as expensive chocolates sent from home. It was done more from tedium and a lack of imagination than malice.

Because a caste system existed within the caste system, I was paired with Mellon. His father had been accused of some sort of fraud. If he had swindled only the poor, I assume his son would have been welcome, and I would have been assigned to someone else. But Mellon père had crossed the line and stolen from the wealthy. When a crime is committed, small or notorious, by someone from a minority, every person of that group squirms with the fear of repercussions beyond and out of proportion with the crime. But at Sunshine their grievance was internal and the result punitive.

Linking us didn't create friendship; official pairs were required during activities such as canoeing, tennis, and deep-water swimming. Mellon is a horrible name for a child who is well liked, let alone someone who is ostracized. At Sunshine, they called him the Lope, as in canta-lope. Even our counselor, Ned, called him the Lope.

Ned, a former camper, possessed a perennial squint that betrayed his anxiety about what people above and around him might be saying. If there had been an organization of junior sycophants, he would have been the first to say yes and join. It must have been hard to go through life always frightened. Ned deeply wanted to inculcate us with the traditions of Sunshine. He did so by repeating his version of the Sunshine motto, "Liberté, égalité, fraternity." Not fraternité but striped-polo-shirts fraternity.

Ned was most serious when completing the nightly KYBO report. Although I never learned the exact meaning of the initials, I thought they stood for "Keep Your Bowels Open" because every night after dinner, Ned would dutifully record our responses to the following questions:

"Did you write home today?"

"Did you excel at anything today?"

And "Did you KYBO today?" referring to a crap.

Just exactly how these activities were related remained unclear to me. Tad and Trey, who were quite regular, took an unnatural interest in each other's bowel movements, which shed light on why Mengele and others liked to study twins. Fortunately, they did not keep an official accounting of how often Mellon masturbated, for which he had a distinct aptitude.

I found it useful to masquerade as a street-tough in order to intimidate Ned and the others. On the days I did not wear my junior wifebeater, I rolled cigarettes in the sleeve of my T-shirt. I always carried my pocketknife and played basic schoolyard basketball by going hard to the hoop no matter who came between me and the bucket. I did not want to get close to anyone and have them ask how Unkle Traktor and Aunt Georgia became my guardians. Nor did I want anyone to learn about their Communist ties or Unkle Traktor's ideological quirks, such as getting unreasonably irritated when someone called him a Trotskyite.

The true benefit of my association with Mellon were the meals. Since his father was still out on bail, his parents often came to visit, and would take us to expensive seafood restaurants with French names. At first I was intimidated. I, a twelve-year-old, was the representative of an entire religion. How was I going to explain why Jews cannot eat this or that, or worse, unravel the logic and history behind Jewish dietary laws? Why, for instance, is the waiting time between eating first dairy then meat different than the waiting time between eating meat then dairy? Or if we are right, how come the entire non-Jewish world is not dead of shrimp or pig poisoning? All Jews, including the ones who do not keep kosher and those who barely know their home address know the spelling and dangers of trichinosis and crustaceans and are imbued with the horrors of eating pork and shellfish.

Add to this, Jews never eat fish in its natural state. It must be smoked, mashed, mushed, pickled, salted, peppered, creamed, or transformed into *gefilte* fish before it can be served. How do you rationally explain that?

I did not recognize the names of any of French fish on the menu, so I ordered something I hoped was not shellfish. I was quite fearful of appearing hypocritical and eating prohibited food that was not Chinese. At least back home, seafood restaurants had landlubber's menus, offering something chicken to acknowledge that the neighborhood had not been redlined. My fish arrived oval except for the tail. It was accompanied by a lonely lemon wedge enrobed in mesh, which I removed as being unnatural. From then on, wherever we went, I ordered sole, which everyone naturally assumed was my favorite. And in a way it was.

Sitting across from Mellon's dour parents, I was so uncomfortable that I passed up a family joke. "I don't see herring on the menu. I guess it is too early for young kippers." Yet Mellon's parents had no inkling of my apprehension. In fact, based on our hesitant and dislocated lunchtime discussions, they seemed to believe we shared common interests.

"We sent Mellon to Eton, one of the finest public schools in England," said Mellon's father.

"Me too. I went to P. S. 225 in Brighton Beach. Very good reading and math scores," I said.

"We spent last summer at the beach in Brighton," said Mellon's mom.

"Me too," I said.

"Have you ever been to England?" asked Mellon's dad.

"Just the New one," I said.

With my three-quarters privilege caveat and, as was the wont at Emma Goldman, I thought I would have to wait on tables and wash dishes. But at Sunshine, young men dressed in white outfits with black belts, pretending to be professional waiters, served our meals on matching plates without any chips. And the Sunshine campers ate with their spines parallel to the backs of the chairs. Seemingly, they took no pleasure in their food, spooning it into their mouths at a swift ninety-degree angle. Although impressive, it was more like a gesture of obedience, like dogs sitting quietly by their bowls until given the signal to eat. We also had people who did our laundry. Everyone had name tags in their clothes except me. Any piece of clothing without a label became mine, no matter the size or sex.

The baseball fields at Sunshine were an exuberant green and limned every morning. They fanatically measured the height of each tennis, volleyball, basketball, and badminton net each day to conform to international standards. The wooden canoes seemed polished and unused. And I imagined they drained the lake every night and scrubbed the ring around the shoreline to get rid of the scum left by the nearby bungalow colony.

The only time the three-quarters privilege was invoked was when everyone, save myself, went horseback riding. I was not totally ignorant of horses. Between the eight lanes of traffic on Ocean Parkway in Brooklyn was a bridle path used mostly by people to walk their dogs, but on occasion a horse and rider would pass. I always liked to see the horses waiting for traffic lights as if they were pedestrians or cars. This was not life as seen in westerns or English movies but Brooklyn-style, where everyone had to stop for people actually earning a living, like driving a cab or truck.

While the others were riding, I spent that time in the infirmary with the nurse with the official designation 'under observation.' Despite Aunt Georgia's admonition about not leaving a written record, I often sent letters to Aunt Tillie. I always felt confident Aunt Tillie would not share my secrets and adolescent idiocies. I was also pretty sure none of my letters, outgoing or incoming, were steamed open to reveal their contents.

> *Dear Aunt Tillie:*
>
> *As you probably know, I am at the wrong camp. I am not at Camp Emma Goldman. I am at Camp Sunshine. It is filled with very rich kids. Some are from important families, they tell me. "Prominent" is what they call it. They tell me prominent is good. It seems that stupid and lazy children from these prominent families are "set for life." Another term I just learned. Please send any Jewish food you think will make it through the mail.*
>
> *PS: I think I found what I want to do with the rest of my life. I want to observe the lives of others and then tell them what I think of their lives.*

Within a week, Aunt Tillie sent me three dozen mon cookies, sugar cookies, but not too sweet, and dotted with thousands of poppy seeds. She attached a note.

> *Be careful with your observations. Remember what happened to Michael Rockefeller.*

That summer, I auditioned for *Guys and Dolls,* Sunshine's main production of the summer. I desperately wanted a role. After all, Abe Burrows, one of the writers of the play, had been denied the Pulitzer Prize because of his troubles with HUAC. A motivation I kept to myself.

Monte was our dramatics counselor. His real name was something like Davey O'Brien, but he chose Monte because he thought it sounded more considerable. He pronounced it "Mon-TAY" to heighten the effect and called himself the theatrical director. It was rumored that Monte had once been a prominent director of Broadway musicals or movies or something. But after he told Gene Kelly that dancing in puddles was stupid, he was relegated to directing people like myself.

It was at these auditions that I first saw Patrice Anne. The sun bounced off her skin like a nomad's white kaftan reflecting the heat. She was as elegant as any fourteen-year-old could be. She parted her strawberry-blonde hair just slightly off-center, so as not to look like a poet. Patrice Anne was exotic. There was no one like her where we lived.

Monte selected me to play the part of Nicely Nicely, and I would sing "Sit Down, You're Rockin' the Boat." He chose Patrice Anne to play the lead, Adelaide.

Every day at rehearsals, I took the opportunity get closer to her, to sit near her, by her, next to her. At our age, this constituted a relationship. A few of the others would pass by and warn her in a stage whisper, "Watch out. He's not one of us," or "I heard he's a Commie." She cared little what the others said, and she saw through my tough guy facade. I slowly came to trust her. She was not only amused by my Brooklyn upbringing but even intrigued. As for me, her stories of the Upper East Side of Manhattan were just as alien, a world like Sunshine but with concrete underfoot.

My value as a mascot was never higher than when Monte realized I could play the guitar and knew enough songs to lead a campfire sing-along. Of course, I had to submit a play list for approval, but I knew my audience.

I was introduced as a Noble Savage and the first Camp Sunshine Fellow. Though I doubt there was ever a second. I played "Greensleeves," "Tom Dooley," and "Michael, Row Your Boat" and planted a few mildly subversive songs: "If I Had a Hammer" and "Puff, the Magic Dragon." Two counselors thought they were cool by putting two fingers to their mouth and making a sucking sound. Nearly everyone sang with a dazed indifference, except Patrice Anne who sang loudly and beautifully.

Someone called out, "You know 'Ain't I Right' by Marty Robbins?"

"Sorry, don't know it," I said.

"Of course you don't," the voice responded.

"Sorry."

"Well, I'm going to sing it, and you can figure out how to play along."

The older brother of one of our Noble Savages, Biff, emerged from the darkness. He walked to the edge of the campfire, his face glowing eerily from the chin up, and he started singing. And not very well. It was more country than anything, but I gamely tried to play along. No one sang with him.

By the time he got to the end of the second verse, he was glaring at me, hoping others would get the message. "Ain't I Right" was not about a wayward grammarian but a gleeful anti-Commie ditty.

I thought this needed a response, so I played "This Land Is Your Land." Woody thought "God Bless America" was exclusive and unrealistic and "This Land" was his antidote. I did not share this bit of subversive history as almost everyone sang the chorus but no one knew the rarely heard verses which I added that night:

As I went walking I saw a sign there
And on the sign it said "No Trespassing."
But on the other side it didn't say nothing,
That side was made for you and me.

In the shadow of the steeple I saw my people,
By the relief office I seen my people;
As they stood there hungry, I stood there asking
Is this land made for you and me?

Biff's older brother and two of his friends waited for me after the sing-along. Apparently their parents were landed developers. They started to shove me and shout, "Commie pinko," and "Jew bastard." Not too bad. Only one Jew bastard the entire summer.

All three were bigger than me. I could have sworn I saw my counselor Ned lurking in the shadows. He knew from which pockets his tips would come.

One aspect of being streetwise is knowing when to fight. Sometimes you have to fight even when you're going to lose. I considered kicking two of them in the balls and gouging the third in the eyes. I could have run and hoped that someone from senior staff would intervene. Then I had a better idea. I pulled out my wallet and managed to find my Republican voter registration card, an ironic family heirloom. Unkle Traktor had found it lying on the ground after a melee at Union Square Park with some outside agitators. He decided that the youngest person in the family should carry it around as a reminder of what not to become. And when my next sibling or cousin turned ten, they would become the temporary holder of the card and so on from generation to generation.

"See, I'm one of you," I said, holding up the card and concealing the real person's name with my finger.

Fortunately, it never dawned on them how or why a twelve-year-old had a Republican voter registration card. All they saw was a tangible representation of their culture.

One of the boys said, "OK. But I have to hit you. I have to be able to tell the others I hit you."

"OK," I said. "But not in the face or the nuts."

Nothing was mentioned at the next rehearsal, and Monte acted as if he was not aware of the fight. But did I share some of Aunt Tillie's constant supply of mon cookies with Patrice Anne. She, in turn, invited me to visit her that very night.

The girls' camp was across the lake. The lake was named after an unknown and unpronounceable Native American, so everyone simply called it the lake. There were three ways to get across the lake—swim, take a canoe, or use the footpath along the shoreline. The inherent dangers in swimming or taking a canoe in the dark allowed for the possibility of death by romance. But everyone used the footpath but never admitted it. Still, apocryphal tales, shrouded in death, arose about crossing the lake at night. Supposedly, a head counselor drowned while heading for a night of debauchery with an underage camper. All of which allowed the kids to say, "Sex kills."

I arrived at Patrice Anne's cabin and tried not to wake the others. We spoke in hushed whispers, smelling of mouthwash. We, of course, discussed how I got across the lake and I lied and said that I had taken a canoe. We gossiped about Monte and the other *Guys and Dolls* cast members and we laughed at things that weren't funny. I wanted to touch her, but her pajamas seemed too expensive. Then she suddenly asked, "You're Jewish, right?"

"Yeah, why?"

"Just curious."

"I am."

"Can you prove it?"

"Sure. Do you want me to recite a blessing?"

"What kind of blessing?"

"Well, we have all sorts of blessings. Mostly about food and death." She saw my hesitation and said, "You know what I mean."

"Not really." I didn't.

"I've never seen a real one."

"A real what?"

"Well, except for my brother's. But that was an accident. And never one with missing pieces."

I was confused for a while, and then I realized what she was saying. "That? You want to see that?"

"Yes, 'that.' Jews have missing pieces, right?"

"Well, some. But not big pieces. I never saw the original. They took it away a long time ago."

"So can I see it? Just once. Please."

Until that moment, I did not think that rich boys' were different than mine. In fact, I had never seen anyone's original. Sex is confusing for many, especially adolescents. And uncertainty can be an effective and primary form of birth control. Patrice Anne was genuinely curious. Maybe I could foster a better understanding between Jews and non-Jews, so as I began fumbling with my pants.

All at once beams from flashlights appeared from every angle all aimed at me. It was as if a prisoner had broken out, and the guards turned on their searchlights and unleashed the dogs. The dark filled with tittering and laughing and random comments.

"Is that what it looks like?"

"I've never seen one like that."

"It is different."

"Kill it before it grows."

"I must find one just like it."

"Let's call him 'Sir Cumcision.' "

I was totally humiliated and felt betrayed by Patrice Anne. I leaped up and ran from her bunkhouse, pulling up my pants, stumbling along the footpath back to the boys' side.

I avoided Patrice Anne the next day, but she insisted I speak with her. She told me over and over that she did not know what the others had planned. She admitted that she had told them that I was coming over but repeated her sincere, teary, and profuse apology. I wanted to believe her but remained unconvinced until that day's rehearsal. Then Patrice Anne had to sing "Adelaide's Lament." From the emotion in her voice and her watery eyes, I understood she was singing to me, the boy with the missing pieces.

For the remainder of the summer, Patrice Anne and I spent as much time together as possible, surreptitiously meeting at the boathouse whenever we could. Our time together and our relationship were frightening, enthralling, confounding, physical, and emotional. I was unprepared in every way, and that made it even more memorable. For all of Patrice Anne's attentiveness, it did not stop the entire camp from calling me Sir Cumcision, or more the terse but ironic Sir.

We only saw each other twice after camp ended, under watchful and disapproving parental eyes. Of course, she has a special page in my life, and I hope for the same in hers.

And before I returned home, I wrote one last letter.

Dear Aunt Tillie:

When I think about the summer, I think the biggest difference between us and them is that we are darker. Jewish people are not exactly white. I don't mean skin color. Our hair is darker, our eyes are darker. When I lie in my bunk in the pitch black, the others seem to glow. You cannot find me. They are confident about the future, but you taught us the Yiddish proverb, "Men plan and God laughs." We also laugh at different things. We laugh at things we are not supposed to, like death and failure, and that only makes it funnier. Our food is darker. They eat white bread, we eat pumpernickel and rye, and we dunk it in soup. We live in neighborhoods with dark-haired neighbors with heavy woolen coats, and we have beauty parlors that turn dark hair into blondes. Even the covers and spines of our most important books are black.

Nobody really wants us because we are just different. We read different books and have different heroes. When we pray, we do not kneel. You always use the word shanda, but there is no such word in English or here. Here they speak about their clothes a lot, and they have many words for the same color: taupe, ecru, shell, off-white, beige, even mushroom. Kind of useless, I guess, but then I thought Jews too are not exactly white but off-white. But I don't think we are taupe.

17

Planning

Fern disguised her true intention when she asked everyone to join her on the patio on Memorial Day.

A few days earlier she visited Herbert Plotnick, who passed his life in one of the warren of offices on Nassau Street. Even though the buildings were taller in other areas of New York, on Nassau Street the air felt thicker, the street darker and narrower, and the light bulbs dimmer. It was forbidden to wash windows. Reminders of WWII in the form of metal-clad windows that prevented light from seeping through during an air raid could still be found. It was the perfect environment to cultivate mushrooms and stamp dealers.

Fern saw a distorted figure through the frosted-glass window framed by his office door and rang the buzzer. Plotnick answered. He was an ordinary-looking sort, save for a large silver ring that glittered like a fishing lure. And while stamp collecting is an innocuous—even sometimes an educational—avocation for most children, the ones who grew up to become stamp dealers were always the last to be chosen when teams were decided and never the ones chosen by the girls. As with many adults who were once the objects of scorn, money, power, and feeble attempts at sexual conquest become their sources of revenge.

"Just a minute," Plotnick said as he turned his back to Fern and closed a safe the size of a coffin, albeit one that stood erect.

"How can I help you?"

"I want to sell you something," said Fern.

"What?"

Every serious collector has a primary interest, but they always have at least one other fascination, if not five or six. From a shopping bag, Fern took out all the dildos and the magazines she told everyone she threw out years ago and unwrapped each one like it mattered. Plotnick's mien changed, and he could not conceal his excitement. "How did you find me?"

"Cohen the jeweler on Fulton Street said you'd be interested."

"Cohen is a traitor and a gonif, and you can tell him I said so."

Plotnick pushed aside the clutter on his desk and laid every dildo out carefully as if preparing sterilized instruments for surgery. He examined each one first through a jeweler's loupe and then through a large hinged magnifying glass on a stand.

"This one appears worn," he said with a sense of titillation. "Did you know the first sex toy was found almost thirty thousand years ago in a cave near Ulm, Germany? Not too far from where my family comes from."

Plotnick went on for a few more instructive moments. "You have here a 1918 Sears Roebuck catalog page. They sold vibrators as vacuum cleaning attachments"—then he added in a highly flawed French—"The first instance in print was probably *Choise of Valentines* or the *Merie Ballad of Nash his Dildo* around 1593."

Most other people read *A Tale of Two Cities* in high school, thought Fern. Plotnick continued, "Companies like General Electric, Oster, and Hamilton-Beach manufactured them under the guise of massage devices, but everybody knew what they were used for." He omitted the phrase "including me."

"But when everybody saw jazz-age porno films, and they were no longer a dirty little secret, they died a public death," he said with an air of resignation. "I'll give you three hundred dollars."

Although Fern was a bit frightened of him, she easily measured Plotnick. "I can see your interest is purely academic, but I want to sell them. So let me take them elsewhere."

"OK, five hundred."

Fern watched him as he almost trembled as he inspected each one, while simultaneously trying to keep a running tabulation of their value.

"These have great sentimental value, and I just want to make sure they find a good home."

"OK, eight hundred."

"Make it a grand, and you have a deal," Fern said, trying not to over-play her hand or his. Fern could see Plotnick hesitate as he was con-flicted by his need to steal and that of satisfying a larger urge.

"A grand and not a penny more," Plotnick said.

"Deal."

Plotnick opened up a smaller safe that was buried under some stamp journals and an estate sale he had yet to sort, and he counted out the money.

On the subway ride home, the wicker subway seat poked Fern in the ass a few times, almost as a reminder of what she had just done. She changed seats as the cane almost tore her stockings and when she settled that second time Fern surreptitiously slipped her hand into her purse to make sure the money was still there.

Fern thought she could never return to Cohen the jeweler, not that there weren't other jewelers, but how did he know about Plotnick? What else did they share? What did he think of her? How come all these escapees from Europe often seemed more worldly, more edu-cated, more sexually open than American Jews? But if she did go back to his store, she would certainly thank him.

"I wonder why Fern called us here," my mother said.

"Maybe Jerry bought a new shirt."

"No, we would have seen that on the news."

"Maybe Yudel got hit by a truck again. A nicer truck."

The patio remained a constant. Although the facade of one of the neighboring apartment buildings had been painted, it still appeared gritty. The family sat in the same order and not in a circle, but in a semicircle like a stage set facing the audience, except the audience in this case was a clothesline.

My father brought a new and much larger hibachi. His first burgers tasted of lighter fluid. My grandmother's mind and cooking ability were still keen, but her knees did not work, and she could not carry what she made down the stairs. For some reason at this stage of her life, she decided that it was not dignified to yell out of the window but tossing each latke as it browned was. She threw them from her second-story kitchen window to the belching seals below as they stared up. Some used their hands, others plates, and others bowls to catch them. My grandmother did not seem a bit concerned she created this Darwinian frenzy. For my father and Tummler it was not who was hungry but who could catch more flying latkes.

Fern, no longer able to contain herself, reached into her purse and fanned a few packs of twenties.

"Here it is. Eight hundred bucks."

"Where did you get that?"

"What are you going to do with that?"

"We're all going to be arrested, aren't we?"

Fern was well aware of the change in attitude toward bar mitzvahs and was trying to gain the advantage. They were pioneers in the movement when bar mitzvahs no longer belonged to the child but to the mother. Family and friends would say they are going to Belle's bar mitzvah or Frieda's bar mitzvah; the child's name was lost in the fog of their need for recognition. The bar mitzvah was now preceded by the mother's name, and I had plenty of mothers. And Fern's intention was to buy her way to the top.

"With this money, I will decide where the bar mitzvah will be and who will be invited."

This was followed by my family's own version of *The Three Bears*, if not eight or twelve bears.

"But he's my natural child," said my natural mother.

"We taught him invaluable lessons about what is important in life," said Aunt Esther.

"You mean like getting blacklisted? We taught him important stuff, too," said Muriel.

"Muriel, do not be distracted by reality," said Uncle Murray.

"Where did you get that money?"

"It doesn't matter, I got it."

At which point another latke came flying out of the window, hitting Tummler in the eye.

"Was it crisp?" asked my father.

Occasionally someone gave one to my grandfather, who preferred to eat his with sour cream instead of applesauce. My mother liked to dip her latkes in both, an odd combination of tastes and swirls.

Each mother at once had both a valid and a worthless claim as to whose bar mitzvah it should be. I did nothing to quell this argument, as the rabbi was not appreciative of my unique approach to my bar mitzvah, and I did not wish to reveal my own conflict. They had all contributed to my education in their own way.

My grandmother did not hear the words, but could hear the distinct rise and fall of voices that constituted a fight. Instead of yelling, she wrote a note, wrapped it in a tissue, added a dime in it, and threw it down, the way she did when my mother and Aunt Esther were small and they wanted to buy ice cream. The note read, "Don't make me come down there." Everything else was implied.

If there is a hierarchy of irrational behavior and its remedy, I have yet to figure it out. What was grandmother going to do? Yell at them? Exile them? Not feed them? What was her power? The family continued to argue in whispers through clenched teeth.

"So you want to throw the party. That's fine," said my mother. "Are you going to cater it with pot cheese from your grocery?"

"That's what the eight hundred bucks is for."

"The actual bar mitzvah is nothing more than a reservation for the party where the rabbi is the maître'd," said my father.

"Who you going to use for music?"

"We could have comics instead of music," said Tummler, "I know a lot of them who could use the work."

"Those comics are out of work for a reason."

"How are you going to dance to a comedian?"

"They can whistle *Hava Negilah*."

"You know, some people keep kosher."

"I never had pot cheese at a bar mitzvah. Or a wedding."

And they hadn't gotten to the most contentious aspects of the party—the candle lighting ceremony and at which tables people should sit. The candle lighting ceremony is supposed to honor venerated friends and family members who light one of the first thirteen candles for the bar mitzvah. The parents light the last one and unless this was resolved, it could be a stampede.

"You know you have to invite Cousin Gertie. She won't come, but she gets angry if she can't say no first," Muriel said.

"To be Jewish now is to be middle class," Uncle Morty said.

"When I was a kid, you mumbled a few words in Hebrew and then you said, 'Today, I am fountain pen,' and you were bar mitzvahed," Tummler said.

"You know muslin boys have their *schvantz* cut off when they are thirteen."

"Muslim, not muslin. Not everyone is in the schmatta business."

"I think the Muslims only do the half schvantz."

"You would think after all the problems in Europe, a bar mitzvah would be something more than a party."

"So," Fern asked, "does my money talk?"

"Be sure it's not the same day as Beatty's son Barry's wedding."

"When is it?"

"I don't know."

"We know what you did with the man with the overcoat when you made him sleep on the dog bed."

"That has nothing to do with the bar mitzvah."

"*Feh* on stuffed derma. Why do they always serve it?"

"You're such a *muzhik*. You don't know what's good."

"Why don't we just order in Chinks?"

"For a hundred and seventy-five people?"

"For once in your life act like *mensch*, Tummler," said Uncle Morty, "It is Chinese, not Chinks, *Chinese*. The world is changing. Would you like it if someone said, "Let's go for kikes?"

"You're an anti-Semite, Traktor," Tummler said.

"I am making an analogy."

"I don't give a damn what you're making, you're an anti-Semite."

"Just stop calling it Chinks."

And into the night.

I learned so much that day. What is important to others is not necessarily to you. The fight often has nothing to do with what they are fighting about. You never know where and when you might learn something. And maybe most important, you do not have to know what you're talking about to be right.

"The onus is on the sane," my father said. "Anyone else want a burger?"

"Is it medium well?"

"Of course."

18

The Rites of Fall

Grout sealed the corners of Rabbi Birnbaum's mouth. More precisely, his denture adhesive oozed from its artificial shell, then cruelly tossed in a sea of platitudes, and beached in the crotch of his lips. There was an odd mesmerizing white elasticity to it.

"What's that between your eyes?" asked Rabbi Birnbaum.

"What's what between my eyes?" I asked in return.

"That mark."

"Oh, the scar. Sometimes I forget it's there."

"It looks like Israel."

"I know, it does looks like Israel. I got it in an accident."

"An accident?"

"Yeah, my cousin Yudel got his fingers chopped off in a bread slicer. He owed the wrong people money. One day, when I was little, he tried to pick me up and, because he had no fingers, I fell right through and he dropped me on my head. So that's how I got a scar that looks like Israel."

"You are being sacrilegious."

"No, Rabbi. I'm telling you the truth."

In our shul, Rabbi Birnbaum presided over the bar mitzvah rites, a costume drama in three acts, the first two in Hebrew. It began with the kid reading selected passages from the Prophets called the *Haftorah*. This name had to be explained to every child since it sounds like half a Torah, which would be a sizeable amount to memorize. Then the bar mitzvah boy reads that week's portion of the Torah, and finally a highly practiced speech in English written by no one in particular and forgotten once it left the tongue.

In preparation for my bar mitzvah, I rehearsed my English speech in a variety of accents. The best versions were Yiddish, Spanish, and a highly exaggerated Brooklyn inflection, basically Jimmy the Hair. The rabbi did not appreciate these variations, nor was he amused by my Jewish auctioneer, where I pretended to sell off portions of the Torah. My western drawl, where I requested a whiskey at the Barrrrr Mitzvah, also drew scowls. I had already been suspended from Hebrew school for scalping tickets for the High Holiday services. "First row. Blow the *shofar*. Check 'em out." Pubescent creativity and tradition are immutable contradictions.

"For someone such as yourself," said the rabbi, "the best way to deliver a speech is with the greatest dignity and sincerity. As much as someone like yourself can muster. Do not race through it. You should proceed thusly. I want you to count one after every comma and two for every period."

"Dearest parents, one, esteemed rabbis, one, assembled family and friends, one, and members of the congregation, two. On this most important day of my life, one, I stand before you, two."

"Not aloud. Silently. Do it again."

Of course, I didn't say anything. The rabbi let several uncomfortable silent moments pass before he said, "Just the numbers. Do not say the numbers aloud. Not the whole speech. Recite it again. Keep the numbers to yourself."

"Are you mocking me, young man? If you don't learn to do this properly, and soon, you are not going to be a bar mitzvah. Do you understand me? Do you want to embarrass your parents? The congregation? ME? He knew a well-placed parable would be wasted and just a few years earlier, he would have slapped me. Do you want me to call your parents or do you want me to cancel your bar mitzvah? Don't tempt me, Mister."

Options as a threat is a venerable Brooklyn tradition and when offered in the streets is at once both cruder and more refined. "Do you want me to take your tongue and pull it out of your ass? Or do you want me to stick your feet on the top of your head and you walk upside down?" I never imagined that even a mild form of threat would penetrate the shul. But knowing the importance of this for my family, I simply tried to learn my lessons.

Traditionally, there have been two types of rabbis. There are the avuncular souls whose analogies and anecdotes make little sense but require a gentle laugh or a quiet nod of acknowledgment by the listener. Then there are those like Rabbi Birnbaum who must have been hung by his *tzitzit* at the seminary.

But the president of the shul decided a third type, a new type, was needed: the hip rabbi. For his first performance, he wore glasses, more for style than for reading the Talmud, his *yarmulke* cocked at a jaunty angle. Rabbi Ringo even wore Cuban stacked-heeled shoes on the *bima* one Saturday morning. Religion was secondary to his attitude. Even as a kid, I never understood dedicating your life to religion, but here was a fellow whose reason for being appeared to defy what he believed and studied. His mere presence stood as an obstacle to believing. It was akin to Wittgenstein repudiating his own theories. Although I found this institutional incongruity magnetic, due to my behavior I was relegated to Rabbi Birnbaum.

On the secular side of preparation for the event, my mother took me to Orchard Street for a suit and then to Klein's on Union Square for a shirt, tie, and clean underwear. The neighborhood tailor made minor alterations to my pants and then asked me to chew on some thread. My father watched proudly throughout. Tummler tried to explain the finer points of delivering a speech, citing his stand-up routine as an example. Muriel repeatedly told me to be sure I had brushed my teeth. She said that the impression I would make on my bar mitzvah would stand until the death of each guest, although most of them hardly knew me anyway.

My family arrived early the Saturday morning of my bar mitzvah. They rarely went to shul and positioned themselves in the third row. They needed clues from the regulars who sat in the first two rows as to when to bend, stand, repeat things, and sing. There was the usual craning of necks to see who entered and decide whether to wave to them, walk over to greet them, give a brief and obvious false smile, or pretend not to recognize them at all.

Aunt Esther and Uncle Morty settled fitfully, fearful of being unmasked as atheists. Skippy/Basil slipped a Bible or two into his coat. Aunt Tillie came with her somewhat dead husband, Willie. Willie was told where to be and when, a life that suited him well. Aunt Tillie did not realize this until after marriage, but it also suited her well. His obsequiousness allowed her a full life in and out of their apartment. Now she sat and fidgeted, knowing my secrets, and the shadows of others.

Patrice Anne sat, hands clasped gracefully, among the gathered faithful of another's religion. Her father had barely stopped his car to drop her off. After seeing our neighborhood, he became more frightened for his car than for his daughter's well-being. He gave her seventy-six dimes in case the phone swallowed the first seventy-five, so she could call if there was an emergency.

Like all pomp and circumstance, my bar mitzvah was preceded by an unnatural silence. I sat on an oversized chair uncomfortable in my new suit and a yarmulke and a *tallit,* gifts of the sisterhood of the shul purchased in bulk for all the bar mitzvah kids. Rabbis Ringo and Birnbaum emerged from their secret back room and dramatically swept across the bima, their tallis flowing behind them as if caught in a draft. With great sobriety, they did this and that until they opened the ark. Everyone rose, and Rabbi Birnbaum removed one of the scrolls of Torah, beautifully adorned in velvet, and an ornate silver and gold breastplate, crown, and shield. The residue of a once wealthy neighborhood.

After the prolonged hush of the ritual and before I recited my portion of the Torah, Rabbi Birnbaum began a desperate and feverish search, he could not find the *yad,* the ornate silver pointer that allows you to follow the text as one reading the Torah for the first time. I, however, proud to improvise, used my disfigured middle finger as a guide. Rabbi Birnbaum thought this was blasphemy, the greatest insult ever delivered by a bar mitzvah and let out a loud, "You *kofer*. You infidel." Due to the tilt of the podium, no one could actually see my profane finger and the congregation only heard what sounded like a moment of unprovoked insanity from Rabbi Birnbaum. I continued reading as if I were the lone pious child in the room. Rabbi Ringo's eyes darted about as he considered the consequences. Perhaps, he thought, he might have found a kindred spirit in me. I might have started a coup against Rabbi Birnbaum, of which he would be the natural beneficiary.

When I finished, Rabbi Birnbaum put his arm around me and jerked us around to face the ark, hissing and spitting in denture adhesive white, "That was heresy. How could you do such a thing?"

"I was born with a finger like that," I said, which was only a few weeks removed from the truth and easier to explain than the curious circumstances of another accident.

"I don't believe you. You'd better bring your medical records to me on Monday. Now behave."

We turned again to face the congregation. I returned to the podium where I read my Haftorah with unexpected perfection. This created an interlude of calm, bordering on palpable spirituality and contorted looks on Rabbis' faces, as they twitched in surprise, appreciation, and confusion.

Rabbi Birnbaum then gave an obligatory sermon laced with platitudes, exhortations, and admonishments, a few of those spears thrown directly at me. And when he was done it was time for my speech. This was probably going to be my last moment in this shul. Maybe any shul.

With my recently acquired dignity, I began my English speech. "Dearest parents (silent one), esteemed rabbis (silent one), assembled family and friends (silent one), and members of the congregation (silent one, two). This very day is dedicated to tradition. Tradition is six thousand years that has led to this glorious morning. (Grandfather.) The exchange between father and son and all his forefathers. (Father)."

But then I became filled with the ambivalence of being both a boy and a man. For the past four years, I attended Hebrew school after public school, every weekday except for Fridays, just for this moment. No matter with whom I lived, I trekked to learn a language for which I had no aptitude, and to learn about a religion and its past, where the mysterious, spiritual, and historical mingled. What could be a greater statement when you join the community as an adult than to state what you think, rather than what is prescribed and practiced?

"But what is a tradition but a mistake made twice. (Aunt Tillie.) Tradition is that half-priced seat behind a pole that only lets you see part of the ball game. (Tummler.) Tradition is also a way to control the proletariat. (Unkle Traktor.) So, what have we learned about tradition? The dead are annoying."

I hesitated. I do not recall whether it was the imaginary footfalls of Rabbi Birnbaum clomping in my direction or the gathered staring back at me with great detachment, but without a proper introduction or provocation I blurted out, "I lost my virginity this summer. To a *shiksa*, a beautiful shiksa." (One. Two. Three. Four.)

There were great gasps, confusion, shouts of derision, and disappointment in many faces but also laughter, indignation, and a smattering of applause. Although slightly red-faced, Patrice Anne smiled sheepishly, staring down at the worn carpet.

The imagined footsteps of Rabbi Birnbaum became real. He steamed in my direction as if the Egyptians had crossed the Suez again. The rabbi lunged at me. I easily eluded the grasp of this angry elderly man. Still I did not want a chase scene around the bima and up and down the aisles. I bent over and said into the microphone, "Thank you, Rabbi Birnbaum, for allowing me to speak freely. I am guessing there are few rabbis who would allow me to say these things. Thank you. Thank you."

"So let us," I continued, "in the weekly tradition of unity and goodwill, wish each other a good Shabbos. Please turn to the one next to you and shake their hand and wish them a 'Good Shabbos.'"

Rabbi Birnbaum had no alternative but to shake my extended hand and wish me a good Shabbos in front of everyone, knowing full well he had just painfully given me and my statements a tacit approbation. Rabbi Ringo appeared by my side. He told me that I should consider becoming a rabbi or perhaps an insurance salesman.

I quietly walked down the steps of the bima into the arms of my family, where my mother waited for me and said, "You should be ashamed. I'm beside myself." My father, resigned to who I was, simply hugged me.

Family members crowded about me. Aunt Tillie said that what I did was both understandable and wrong, without indicating which comments fell on what side of her moral ambiguity.

Skippy/Basil said nothing but briefly touched my shoulder, in what can be only described as his grandest gesture of affection. Jane, who I had not seen since her return from India, smiled and told me I was wonderful as she placed her palms together in front of her chest.

Tummler said, "Relentlessly funny. A buffo performance," as if my bar mitzvah would appear in *Variety*. He was interrupted by my grandfather who told me, "Today you are a man."

Tummler elbowed ahead of my blind grandfather so he could finish his gig, "In my day we said, 'Today you are a fountain pen.' No one had money, so we all got pens. What the hell a thirteen-year-old does with all those fountain pens is beyond me."

Muriel wedged herself between Tummler and me, "God is going to strike you dead. So I'm going to wait in the hall. God doesn't like to strike people dead in small places."

I was secretly pleased that the rabbi interrupted my speech, for I had nothing else to add. I would never see either Rabbi Birnbaum or Ringo again. Nor Patrice Anne. My only regret of the day. But when you are thirteen, you cannot be sure whether you lost your virginity or just your pants.

The party that followed was held at the Knights of Pythias hall, a once-secret national fraternal group that only allowed entry to able-bodied men who believed in a Supreme Being and who called their lodges "castles." In our neighborhood, the Knights of Pythias was a predominantly Jewish organization, evidenced by the portraits of past lodge commanders nailed to the buckling pressed-wood paneling. In many photos taken at that party, those framed faces appeared like ghosts in suits and ties floating over the shoulders of the guests.

An overdressed bar mitzvah band played some big-band arrangements, corny hokey-pokey numbers, and a defanged version of *Tutti Frutti* that had made Pat Boone sound like he was blacker and gayer than Little Richard. The clarinetist saved the day by blowing a rousing klezmer rendition of *Hava Nagila* compelling many to wildly dance the hora. Others stood near the fringes of the circle clapping and yelling encouragement. Muriel said to no one in particular, "My feet hurt just from watching the fakakta dance."

Of course, Fern was in charge of the party. She controlled the band and sang four or five numbers, which may have been her sole intention from the start. She lorded over the large folding tables covered with lopsided aluminum pans of stuffed derma, franks in blankets, and miniature knishes, all heated by Sterno cans blazing an inch above the paper table cloths. The guests loaded their plates, glancing sideways to see who piled on more.

Fern wanted a more competitive bar mitzvah party of which she could brag about for years. She would distort, as necessary, the usual measurements of how many people attended, the amount of gifts, the food served, the entertainment, and even create an imaginary celebrity attendee, in order to impress.

Someone told me I had bad breath. Another told me that he admired my speech. Another said that I was a disgrace. The families who had raised me were distracted by people they had not seen in a while and did not cavil. As usual at bar mitzvahs and weddings, there were those who seemingly lived for these events, the type who thought junk mail was specifically mailed to them. Others grabbed the opportunity to tell the same story to anyone willing to listen.

Kids scrupulously avoided the cheek pinchers and anyone playing the "Remember me?" game. Some tried to cajole adults into giving them nips of alcohol while others ran and screamed between the dancers. Mothers admonished them, "Don't be a *vilda chaye,*" as if it would have some effect.

When all the guests were gone, my family divided up the remaining food. Tummler "Hey, Traktor, where are the fuckin' french fries?" The only paid employee of the lodge closed the tables and swept under people's feet. A good time was had by some.

We retreated to my grandmother's house to tally the gifts and discuss what to do with the money. My grandmother took me aside and said, "What you said today was not part of my plan."

"I don't want to be rude, Bubbe," I said, "but I never knew what your plan was."

"Well, whatever you thought it was, that was not part of it."

I did not answer her. But from that day on, I chose with which family to stay.

Glossary

Please note that spoken Yiddish is a conglomeration of languages with a German base. There are also different pronunciations and idioms depending on the geographical origin of the word. Written Yiddish uses Hebrew characters. Thus from Yiddish to English is a transliteration, so others may disagree with the following spellings. Unless specified, the defined words are Yiddish.

bar/baht mitzvah. *Bar* means son and *baht* means daughter and *mitzvah*, in this case, means commandment or law. Depending on the type of Judaism, at the age of thirteen for boys and twelve or thirteen for girls, they become responsible for their actions and members of the adult community. Some non-Jews have the misconception that this is when a Jewish boy is circumcised. (Hebrew)

bima. In Asheknazi synagogues, it is a raised platform with a reading desk. (Hebrew)

bohker. A boy, one who usually attends a yeshiva.

boychik. A term of affection for a young male.

bris. Ceremony where a Jewish male baby is circumcised. (Hebrew)

bubbe. Grandmother.

bubbe meises. Old wives' tales.

chazzer. A pig.

dreck. Shit.

dybbuk. A malicious spirit that possesses the soul of a living being.

fakakta. Something that's not working or real crap.

faygeleh. A gay male (literally a little bird).

feh. A one-word expression that expresses disgust.

fershtay. Capeesh.

fonfered. Mumbled or unintelligible speech.

Futz in dayn gorgel. A curse. "I fart in your throat."

gay avek. Go away.

gay cocken offen yom. Go shit in the ocean.

gefilte fish. Traditionally carp, pike, mullet or whitefish ground with eggs, onion, matzoh meal, and spices to produce a paste or dough, which is then boiled in fish stock. It is as good or bad as it sounds.

genug. Enough already.

gonif. A thief, chiseler.

Gornisht. Nothing.

Gornisht helfin. Beyond nothing.

gotkas. Men's underwear but generally used for all underwear.

Guttenyu. Oh my God.

goyisha. Slightly derogatory word for someone (or something) who is not Jewish.

Haftorah. A selection from part of the Torah called Prophets that is read in synagogue and usually illuminates that portion of the Torah that precedes it. (Hebrew)

halz. Throat.

kapo. A prisoner a concentration camp who acted as a trustee, but the word is synonymous with traitor to the Jews. (German)

kazatsky. A lively dance.

kishka. Beef intestines, usually stuffed with matzoh meal, spices, and fat. Also known as stuffed derma.

kofer. Infidel. (Hebrew)

kuchaleins. Jewish bungalows in the Catskills where people would cook for themselves.

latke. A fried potato pancake made with matzoh meal.

macher. A big shot.

meshugga. Crazy.

mezuzah. Jewish prayer, usually inside a decorative box that is affixed outside the front door and most rooms in the house. (Hebrew)

mohel. A Jewish official who performs the bris. (Hebrew)

mon. Poppy seeds.

muzhik. A derogatory word for peasant (Russian).

Nu. A question. "Well? So tell me already."

Omein. A variation of amen (Hebrew).

payess. Hair that grows into ringlets, where other men would have sideburns (Hebrew).

pishechtz. Urine.

pletzel. A dinner-plate–size bialy.

ruhkes. Ghosts.

schlub. An untalented or unattractive (or both) person.

schmatta. Rag.

schmekel. Penis.

schmuck. An idiot, but literally a penis. (There are lot of words for penis in Yiddish.)

schnorrer. A human sponge.

schvantz. Penis.

sha. Be quiet.

shanda. A shame, a scandal. To do something embarrassing to Jews where non-Jews can observe it.

shtetl. Real and mythical little towns where Jews lived in Eastern Europe, often in poverty.

shikker. A drunkard.

shiksa. A non-Jewish female.

shiva. The seven-day ritual period of mourning with many customs. Many modern Jews do not adhere to all the customs.

shofar. Traditionally a ram's horn that is blown during Rosh Hashanah and Yom Kippur services.

shtarker. Tough guy.

shtetl. Real and mythical little towns where Jews lived in Eastern Europe, often in poverty.

shtup. To fuck.

shul. Jewish temple; the word literally means school.

tallit. Prayer shawl (Hebrew).

tchotchke. A knickknack, usually something of no monetary value but might have sentimental value.

tzitzit. Fringes that hang from the prayer shawl (Hebrew).

vilda chaye. A wild animal, usually said to or about someone who is out of control.

yad. Ornamental pointer used to follow the reading of the Torah (Hebrew).

yahrzeit. The anniversary of a death, very often commemorated by lighting a twenty-four-hour candle. The glass from the yahrzeit candle is then often used for daily use for drinking (Hebrew).

yarmulke. Skullcap (Hebrew).

yenta. A gossip.

zayda. Grandfather.

zetz. A smack, usually to the head.

Made in the USA
Middletown, DE
10 November 2018